STOLEN

The Case of the Irish Crown Jewels

Dear Risa

I wish you
all the best .

Malcolm Mahr

Vero Beach, FL 32967
TCP 27@aol.com

ISBN:

Printed in the United States of America

Dedicated to my dear friend

Miriam Copple

celebrating her 100th birthday.

June 29, 2025

ALSO BY MALCOLM MAHR

HISTORICAL FICTION

The DaVinci Deception
Honjo
The Secret Diary of Marco Polo
The Florentine Diamond
Sandbag Castle
The Golden Madonna
The Outsider
Whisper of the Spirit
The Green House Murders
The Orange Blossom Mob
Shadows in the Swamp

ADDITIONAL MYSTERY NOVELS

Murder at the Paradise Spa
The Boy with A Pipe
The Einstein Project
The Return of the Scorpion
The Hostage
No Man's Land
The Phenomenon

NONFICTION

How to Win in the Yellow Pages.
What Makes a Marriage Work?
You're Retired Now. Relax.

"Sodom and Gomorrah were destroyed by fire, but Dublin Castle still stands."

—New York *Gaelic American,* 4 July 1908

...General Information

IN 1907, IRELAND, A LAND DEEPLY DIVIDED, both politically and socially, reflected the tensions that would shape its history in the 20th century. These divisions were rooted in a complex interplay of identity, religion, economics, and politics.

The question of Ireland's political future dominated discourse. Nationalists, led primarily by the Irish Parliamentary Party, sought Home Rule—not total independence, but a self-governing parliament of their own to handle domestic affairs.

Unionists, particularly concentrated in the northern province of Ulster, vehemently opposed this, fearing economic decline and loss of connection to Britain.

Religious affiliation often aligned with political loyalties. Catholics, who made up most of the population, generally supported Home Rule. Protestants, a minority but dominant in parts of Ulster, were staunchly Unionist. Wealth disparity further exacerbated tensions. Landowners and industrialists, often Protestant, held significant power, while many Catholics lived in poverty as tenant farmers or laborers.

Dublin had its fair share of political agitators in 1907. Organizations like the Gaelic League, the Gaelic Athletic Association, and the Bráithreachas Phoblacht na hÉireann, a secret oath-bound fraternal organization, sought to reclaim Irish identity, often seen as a counterpoint to British cultural dominance.

To many British observers, the Irish were a graceless and insubordinate lot. Unionism was an exclusively Northern Irish phenomenon. The most visible representative of the

British monarchy in Ireland in 1907 was the Lord Lieutenant, also known as the Viceroy, the Liberal peer John Campbell Gordon, Lord Aberdeen.

In that year, Ireland stood at a crossroads, its divisions both a source of conflict and a prelude to transformation. The forces of nationalism, unionism, and social change would soon converge, reshaping the island's destiny in the years to come.

"MY GOD...THE JEWELS ARE GONE."

—Sir Arthur Vicars, Ulster King of Arms

...Prologue

The Jewel Robbery at Dublin Castle

The headquarters of the Dublin Metropolitan Police, the headquarters of the Royal Irish Constabulary, and the head office of the Dublin military garrison are all within a radius of fifty yards of the safe in the Office of Arms. In a word, there is no spot in Dublin, or possibly in the United Kingdom, which at all hours of the twenty-four, is more constantly occupied by soldiers and policemen... Some person got access to the safe and escaped without leaving any trace.

—*The Irish Times*, 9 July 1907

...Introduction

DUBLIN, IRELAND, 1907, a city divided economically and politically, was getting ready for the imminent visit of King Edward VII. Days before the crucial visit, the Irish Crown Jewels mysteriously went missing.

DUBLIN METROPOLITAN POLICE.

DETECTIVE DEPARTMENT,
EXCHANGE COURT,
DUBLIN, 8th July, 1907.

STOLEN

From a Safe in the Office of Arms, Dublin Castle, during the past month, supposed by means of a false key.

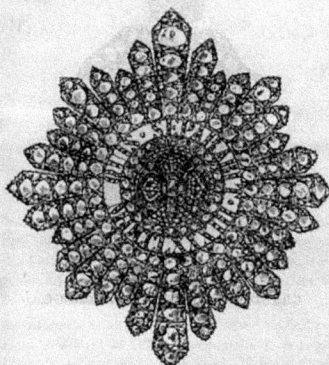

GRAND MASTER'S DIAMOND STAR.

A Diamond Star of the Grand Master of the Order of St. Patrick composed of brilliants (Brazilian stones) of the purest water, 4¼ by 4¼ inches, consisting of eight points, four greater and four lesser, issuing from a centre enclosing a cross of rubies and a trefoil of emeralds surrounding a sky blue enamel circle with words, "Quis Separabit MDCCLXXXIII." in rose diamonds engraved on back. Value about £14,000.

These jewels, formally known as the Regalia of the Order of St. Patrick, were used during state ceremonies to honor knights of the Order. They were stored in Dublin Castle, which served as the seat of British administration in Ireland at the time.

After the theft, in the ensuing investigations, suspicions were rife, and theories proliferated. The police believed it to be an inside job, and the investigation led to a web of political and sexual intrigue that came dangerously close to the Crown itself.

Any crime among the poor was paraded and magnified, but anything connected to the King was treated as sacrosanct, and any word infringing upon it was ruthlessly suppressed. The government's tactics eventually worked. All documents were covered by the British Official Secrecy Act.

The stories eventually faded out of the headlines. The reward was never claimed. And the jewels remain missing, over a century later.

PART I

THEFT AND INVESTIGATION

...1

THE JOURNALIST

MEGHAN WALSH (nee Meghan O'Hara) was born in Glenageary, South Dublin, in 1990, an only child. Her father, Kevin O'Hara, was an intrepid crime reporter for *The Irish Times*. He had been warned, and had been shot at on one occasion, then wounded by gunfire on another, because of his incisive, continuing investigation into Ireland's criminal underworld. On 14 May 2007, Kevin O'Hara was killed by assailants on a motorcycle as he stopped his car at a traffic light in Dublin.

Kevin O'Hara was buried with the rites reserved for a national hero, with the Lord Mayor of Dublin and members of the counsel in attendance, along with his 17-year-old daughter, Meghan, and his wife, Bridget.

Meghan developed a taste for writing after her father died. She became a regular contributor to the letter pages of *The Evening Herald*. By 18 she obtained a weekend job with the paper, writing local crime reports. She studied law for a year at University College in Dublin before leaving to work for *The Herald*.

In 2014 Meghan married her husband, Matthew Walsh, a foreign correspondent for *The Irish Times* covering Asia. He developed a terminal illness, and Meghan relinquished her job to look after him. Following his death, she was invited to work for *The Irish Times* as an investigative journalist.

In 2018, Meghan Walsh and the managing director of *The Irish Times* were prosecuted for offending the Official

Secrets Act. Meghan Walsh was imprisoned after she wrote a story revealing that police had prior knowledge of the robbery of cash from the College Green cash center of the Bank of Ireland in Dublin. It was the largest bank robbery in Ireland's history. The police denied the charge. The judge gave the director, Brendan McFarlane, a hundred-quid fine. Meghan was imprisoned for a term of six months.

After serving her six months in prison, Meghan aspired to be a serious author. Her prime time for writing was in the morning hours. In the afternoon she worked for *The Irish Times*, covering criminal proceedings in Dublin's District Court. For her "day job" stories, the payment typically ranged between 50 to 100 pounds, with higher commissions possible for feature pieces.

The House of Sleep was Meghan's first non-fiction book, published in 2023. Her investigative story concerned the lack of activities, poor nutritional care, and severe fire safety concerns in certain Dublin nursing homes.

In one home, Meghan wrote, "Older people were not provided with any activities. I found residents sitting in rows of seats, with their backs to other residents, facing a television that was not turned on."

Her book won second place in the Women's Prize for Non-Fiction that year in the An Post Irish Book Awards, which celebrated non-fiction written by Irish women. These awards were given annually to authors in various categories, including the Non-Fiction Book of the Year. It was the only literary award supported by all Irish bookstores. The prize recognized excellence in writing, research, and accessibility. The winner received €30,000. Meghan Walsh was awarded second place and a certificate.

She was hard-headed and impulsive, but determined that her next non-fiction book would be good enough to win first place. Meghan's challenge was to pick a topic that would merit the prize. One afternoon while searching the *Irish Time* files, she discovered an interesting article from January 2020.

Sotheby's Sale Stirs Memories of Unsolved Theft of the Irish Crown Jewels

The sale of a "breast star" of the Order of St. Patrick at Sotheby's in London last week cast a long shadow back to Saturday, July 6, 1907, when the Irish Crown Jewels were stolen. The St. Patrick "breast star" refers to the decorative jeweled insignia worn by knights of the Order of St. Patrick, an Irish order of chivalry established by King George III in 1783. The Sotheby's sale item was considered historically significant due to the fact that the original Crown Jewels were stolen and never recovered.

This "breast star" was not part of the Irish Crown Jewels that were stolen. The "breast star," which belonged to the 3rd Lord Oranmore and Browne, was sold for £199,500 ($336,879). It stirred memories of the theft.

This 1907 robbery made world headlines. Also missing were the Diamond Star of St. Patrick and the Collar of the Order, which was a collection of gold roses strung together in a chain, with an imperial jeweled crown at its center with a harp of gold hanging beneath it. Five collars of Knights Companions also disappeared.

At the center of the drama was the Ulster King of Arms, Sir Arthur Vicars, who was responsible for protecting the jewels. No one knew for sure when the theft had taken place, who was responsible, or what had happened to the elaborate gold and jeweled regalia said to be worth today 2,500,000 in pound sterling. The Official Secrets Act caused all documents involved to be restricted. The jewels have never been recovered. To this day, the Irish Crown Jewels remain lost and the mystery unsolved.

...2

WORK-IN-PROGRESS

MEGHAN WALSH WANTED TO PURSUE the Irish Crown Jewels mystery, but with the Official Secrets Act protecting all the background information, she didn't intend to spend another six months in prison. Fortunately, on 5 July 2024, Sir Keir Starmer was appointed prime minister by King Charles III, becoming the first Labour prime minister. Asked about the secrecy acts, the new prime minister said, "The Official Secrets Acts of 1911 provided the main legal protection in the UK against unauthorized disclosure of information relative to the Crown. Events that happened over a hundred years ago should no longer be protected in 2024. I do not want to see anything interrupt good journalism and public interest."

As a result of Sir Keir Starmer's directive, Meghan Walsh found the protected material now available: the reports of the Vice-Regal Commission, Superintendent John Lowe's report on the robbery to the Chief Secretary for Ireland, and the Journals of Dublin's Metropolitan Police Sergeant Owen Kerr, which were replicated in full. However, Scotland Yard Inspector John Kane's official report could never be found.

With all the lords, sirs, police officials, and suspects included in the investigation and Vice-Regal Commission inquiry, Meghan printed a *Who's Who* list and placed it next to her computer.

ARGYLL, Duke of:
>Married to Princess Louise, sister of King Edward VII

ABERDEEN, Lord:
>John C. Gordon (King's representative in Ireland)

BIRRELL, Augustine:
>Chief Secretary for Ireland. Member of British cabinet

BURTCHAELL, George:
>Office of Arms Secretary

EDWARD VII:
>King of Great Britain, Ireland and British dominions

GOLDNEY, Francis:
>Athlone Pursuivant, Mayor of Canterbury

GORGES, Richard:
>Militia Captain

HADDO, Lord George:
>Son of Lord Aberdeen

HARREL, Sir David:
>Assistant Superintendent of the Dublin Police

KANE, John:
>Chief Inspector of the London Police, Scotland Yard

KERR, Owen:
>Detective Sergeant, Dublin Metropolitan Police

LOWE, John:
>Superintendent, Dublin Metropolitan Police

MAHONEY, Pierce Gun:
>The Cork Herald and nephew of Sir Arthur Vicars

O'FARRELL, Mary:
>Office of Arms cleaner

O'MAHONEY, Perce Charles:
>The half-brother of Sir Arthur Vicars

ROSS, Sir John:
>   Commissioner, Dublin Metropolitan Police

SHACKLETON, Francis:
>   Dublin Herald

STIVEY, William:
>   Office of Arms messenger

VICARS, Arthur:
>   Ulster King of Arms

The first item she reviewed was the journals of Sergeant Kerr.

PART II

JOURNALS OF SERGEANT KERR

3

JOURNAL #1—DISCOVERY OF THE THEFT

07 July 1907

MY NAME IS DETECTIVE SERGEANT OWEN KERR of the Dublin Metropolitan Police. I first heard the news of the theft in the early afternoon on Saturday, 06 July, from William Stivey, the Office of Arms messenger. I hurried over to his office and found Assistant Commissioner Sir David Harrel and Sir John Lowe, Superintendent of our Dublin police, present. These two men were my superior officers. There was more purpose to my being called there, because I was the officer who made the tour of inspection each night at the Office of Arms. In a sense, the robbery was on my watch.

Also in the room were both Sir Arthur Vicars and William Stivey. Vicars was not an impressive man physically; small and thin, with light wispy hair worn parted in the center and a mustache curled at both ends.

Vicars said to Superintendent Lowe, "This is the fault of the Board of Works. I asked them for a safe in the strongroom and they did not give it; if they had, this would not have happened."

At four o'clock yesterday, my boss, Commissioner John Ross, had arrived. Vicars went over his story again. Superintendent Lowe interrupted and began to question Vicars about the keys to the safe. "There were two," Vicars answered, "the one that I handed to Stivey, and a spare that I kept at home, safely concealed in my desk."

Vicars next began to cast doubts about the safe in the library. "It was a Ratner model, made by Ratcliff and Homer, and I had been unsure of its effectiveness."

He referred to the lock on the strongroom door. "This particular lock is a Milner, and I have implicit confidence in it."

Sir John Lowe seemed to be satisfied with Vicars's response. Lowe began examining the safe. Sir David Harrel asked when Vicars had last seen the jewels.

"I believe I showed them to a friend, J.C. Hodgson, librarian to the Duke of Northumberland."

"When?" asked Harrel.

"I'm not sure," Vicars admitted.

As an afterthought, Harrel asked Vicars if he had any suggestions to offer as to who might have committed the crime. Then Vicars began to spread the burden of culpability. In response to Harrel's question, he singled out me as the officer who checked the Office of Arms at night.

Sir John Ross ignored Vicars's comment. "Yes, we understand Detective Kerr was on duty on Saturday night," he said. "Do you have any other suspects?"

"My own coachman, Phillips," Vicars added. "He had access to my keys. On one occasion, he had even brought them from Clonskeagh to the castle when they had been left behind—and, well, he was not a gentleman."

I thought Vicars's shabby treatment of me, and Phillips, reflected little credit upon him. He was desperately seeking to protect himself. Now it seemed William Stivey, his messenger, suddenly came to life. Perhaps Stivey was watching the blame being spread, none too skillfully, by Vicars, and wondered how long it would be before some adhered to him as the Office of Arms messenger. He told the officers, "Though I am here for six year, I've never had the key in my hand before."

John Lowe asked Sir Arthur Vicars, "Is this account truthful?"

Vickers gave Stivey a dark look. "Yes. That is so. I was pressured with business, and I sent Stivey with the key, but I was coming immediately after him."

Frustration etched into Superintendent Lowe's face. He mumbled, "Holy Mother of God, the King is coming to Dublin in four days. Who will tell him the Crown Jewels were stolen?"

4

JOURNAL #2—INVESTIGATION

08 July 1907

I BREATHED A DEEP SIGH as I entered the castle for my scheduled meeting with my commissioner. The jewels were missing on my watch. My police career could be over.

Sir John Ross allowed himself a hard smile. "This robbery is a challenge, a real bloody challenge. No forced entry. No sentries reported anything strange on Saturday night. David Harrel and John Lowe suspect you, but they concede that evidence is thin. Their theory requires a man who could go into the Office of Arms with total impunity, and you fit the prescription perfectly."

Inclined to protest, I said nothing.

"Further," Ross told me, "they cannot conceive of a thief wandering around late at night and entering the building. The constable on duty in the Upper Yard would have taken great interest if someone had lit the gas lights in the Office of Arms. He would have become curious and checked things out."

Sir John Ross couldn't contain a faint smile. "I know you're a good detective, but I need to ask: did you steal the Crown Jewels, son? Tell me the truth. Or were you involved with anyone who did?"

"No way," I told Ross. "I made my inspection of the castle offices on Saturday, just as on every other night of the week. My itinerary never varied. I searched the State Apartment shortly after five thirty and the Office of Arms about an hour later."

"I trust you, Kerr. But if you ever prove me wrong, it's the end of my career." Ross kept his expression stony. "And—I'll hunt you down."

"I pledge to you, sir," I said. "It won't come to that."

"Very well. We need to prove Lowe and Harrel wrong by investigating possible witnesses. I want you to start today with William Stivey, the office messenger. He will know who visits the Office of Arms. See where that goes and advise me."

"Will do, sir."

"Then on Monday, bring in the Milner Safe Company. This will do for now. Get busy, and report to me."

*   *   *

LATER THAT MORNING, I was able to interview Mr. William Stivey. I said, "With the Crown Jewels gone and the King visiting Dublin, I've been ordered to interview all possible witnesses, and you're the messenger in the Office of Arms."

"I'll tell you all I can remember, Sergeant."

"Start on Saturday, please." I took out my notebook.

"About twenty minutes past ten, I arrived at the Office of Arms, and I read Mrs. O'Farrell's note. She felt someone had tampered with the strongroom door. I distinctly remembered locking the door on Friday night and seeing everything was as it should have been. Nothing had been touched."

I said, "Please go on."

"At eleven o'clock on Saturday, a package was delivered from West's Jewelers containing the gold collar that belonged to the late Lord de Ros. De Ros had been a Knight of St. Patrick, and his name was to be engraved on it. The package I left on Sir Arthur's desk for his inspection."

17

Stivey hesitated, then he said, "When Sir Arthur reached the Office of Arms around midday, I told him I found a note on my table from Mrs. O'Farrell telling me she had found the strongroom door open.

"'Is that so?' Vicars said, and then walked past me up the stairs to his office."

"How did that make you feel, Mr. Stivey?"

"I was taken aback at Vicars's indifference. The fact that the strongroom door had been found open deserved a less dismissive response. Early in my life," Stivey said, "I was in the Navy and conscious of chains of command, of what happens to subordinates who take unwelcome unnecessary initiatives."

I nodded. "I can agree with that."

"At two fifteen," Stivey continued, "I decided my day's work was done. It was my long-established custom to leave early on Saturdays. But, with the King coming, I made a trip upstairs to see if Vicars need me for anything.

"Sir Arthur handed me the package that had arrived that morning from West's Jewelers. He asked me to take the collar and put it in the safe. Then he reached into his pocket and produced a bunch of keys and indicated the key of the safe and handed it to me. I was astonished. I had never been asked to open the safe.

"When I got there, I found the safe already opened. I took the key from the lock, grabbed the collar box and started back up the stairs. This time Vicars would need to listen to me. By the time I got to the bottom of the stairs, Vicars had already reached the landing and was on his way down. I was relieved; clearly, he had common sense and was coming to supervise me. 'Sir Arthur,' I said. 'I found the safe door unlocked.'

"He asked me, 'What are you saying?' Then Vicars took my keys, went into the library, and opened the safe. At first glance, everything seemed intact. Then Sir Arthur Vicars checked the box that contained the Grand Master's Insignia, the Crown Jewels. It was empty. The man stared at it for a moment, then he shouted, 'My God. They are gone. The jewels are gone.'"

"What happed next?"

"Vicars raced upstairs to tell the office staff about the robbery. I don't know who else he called. I waited half an hour, then I called you, Detective."

"Who else had the keys to the safe and the strongroom?" I asked.

"There are two keys to the safe. Sir Arthur Vicars has them both. There are four keys to the strongroom door, one which had been kept by Sir Arthur himself; one by Mr. Mahoney, the Cork Herald; one with Mr. Burtchaell, the Office of Arms Secretary; and one with me. There is another one locked up in the strongroom itself."

"Can anyone enter the Office of Arms at will?"

At first Stivey was very quiet, then he said, "Admission is only gained to this office by a door from the Upper Castle Yard, which is opened from outside during the day by turning the handle. My room is in proximity. It appears improbable that any person could enter without my knowledge."

"How about after you leave?"

"After hours the office door is always kept locked. A few people have keys and can gain access outside office hours: Sir Arthur himself; the Board of Works Overseer, John O'Keefe, who lights the Tower clock; myself; and Mrs. Mary O'Farrell."

I marked all the names in my book. "Thank you for your honesty."

"One more thing, Detective," Stivey said quietly with a nervous smile. "You best talk to the cleaning lady, Mary O'Farrell. She knows many... things."

*   *   *

THAT NIGHT, I FOLLOWED the advice of Stivey and visited the home of Mary O'Farrell. Although I never suspected her in the theft, I interrogated Mary aggressively. I needed information to deflect Lowe's and Harrel's suspicion. Utterly intimidated, Mrs. O'Farrell told me everything she knew. She told me about finding the strongroom ajar on Saturday morning.

I took out my notebook again. "Go over what happened."

"At about 6:30 a.m.," she said, "I took my route to the castle, walking down Capel Street and crossing the Liffey at Essex Bridge to enter by the Main Gate. Neither the sentries nor the policemen guarding the gate never bothered me none, because they know I always go there six days a week."

I said, "Tell me what happened after you got there."

Mrs. O'Farrell's eyebrows lifted just a touch. She said, "I went straight over to Mr. Stivey's desk to check for any notes from Sir Arthur or any other member of the staff. No notes that day. But as I turned to leave, I saw something that alarmed me. The door of the strongroom was open. Although the office was quiet, it occurred to me that there might be someone inside the room. I listened, but still there wasn't a sound.

"Finally, I checked, and the key was in place. I had no key of my own to lock the strongroom door, but I couldn't just leave the door half open with the key in its lock. I took the key and banged the door shut. After I had finished my cleaning, I settled in to wait for Mr. Stivey. Eventually, I got tired of waiting and scribbled out a note to him that I had found the strongroom door opened this morning. I wrote that I closed it and put the key on his desk. With that, I left."

I closed my notebook and asked, "Anything else?"

Her breath caught in her throat. Hesitantly, she said, "Well, yes, sir."

But the other piece of information confused me. She said, "Some months earlier, in February or March, when I had been cleaning upstairs early, I heard the front door of the tower open. I went downstairs to investigate. The door of the library was open, and a man was standing in front of me. He seemed confused, muttered something about leaving a note on the table in the library, and then left.

"Then I checked the office front door. It was closed and locked. There was no sign that the door had been forced in any way. It dawned on me that the mysterious visitor had been able to let himself in. He had had his own latchkey."

"What did you do?" I asked her.

"I waited to break the news to Mr. Stivey, but that was the last I ever heard of the incident."

"There was never any follow-up inquiry of any kind despite the presence of an intruder in the Bedford Tower?"

"None that I knew of."

I sensed Mary O'Farrell had more to say. "What else can you tell me?"

She nodded. "I'm not certain, but I thought I recognized the man."

"Who?" I asked.

"Lord Haddo," she replied.

*   *   *

21

I WENT BACK TO HEADQUARTERS. Assistant Police Commissioner Harrel was huddled with Sir John Ross. Harrel was over six feet tall and running slightly to fat. He wasn't pleased to see me.

John Ross's gray eyes were calm, but not the note in his voice. "What have you got, Kerr?"

I took a deep breath and told him, "I have a list of suspects who had the safe keys and the strongroom keys, and there are three or four people who could get into the Office of Arms after five or six o'clock."

"Let me see the list," Sir David Harrel said.

As he stared at my report, he said, "Hold on. You have Lord Haddo here."

"Yes, sir," I said. "I interviewed Mary O'Farrell, the cleaning woman. She told me in February or March she was cleaning upstairs in the office when she heard the front door of the tower open and went downstairs to investigate. The door of the library was open, and a man was standing in front of her. Mrs. O'Farrell said she thought she recognized the man; it was Lord Haddo."

"Don't tell me it was Haddo," Harrel snorted. "Lord Aberdeen's son. Scratch his name. We can't have it. Aberdeen is the King's Viceroy."

Ross cut in, "Are you certain she recognized Lord Haddo?"

I answered, "Almost certainly."

"Almost certainly." Harrel moved to retrieve the situation. A grin creased his wide pink face. "Go back to that cleaning person and tell her you investigated the situation. As Chamberlain-in-Waiting, Lord Haddo had been sent to the Office of Arms with a message from his father. Then tell her if she still wants her cleaning job, she will never... ever remember a *visitor.*"

Then Harrel turned to me sharply. He said, "Go on, Kerr, talk to the woman, and try not to bungle *this* one." Commissioner John Ross made no response, because Sir David Harrel outranked him. I remembered what William Stivey had said earlier that day: "Be conscious of chains of command, of what happens to subordinates who take unwelcome initiatives."

"Yes, sir," I said to that fat bastard.

JOURNAL #3—THE ULSTER KING OF ARMS

09 July 1907

I ACCOMPANIED COMMISSIONER ROSS to the Office of Arms at eleven o'clock to see Sir Arthur Vicars, the Ulster King of Arms. Vicars wasn't there. We waited impatiently for over an hour in the Bedford Tower Library in Dublin Castle.

Before noon Sir Arthur Vicars strode into the office. With a painful edge to his voice, he invited us into his office on the second floor. The office was spacious and well-appointed, with dark wood paneling around the walls and two windows facing out onto the Upper Castle Yard.

Once again Sir Arthur recounted how the robbery had been discovered, but now he was apportioning blame. "This is the fault of the Board of Works," he sniffed. "I asked them for a safe in the strongroom, and they didn't give it to me. The door was too small."

"I understand that," Ross said bluntly. "When were the jewels last seen in the safe, Sir Arthur?"

"Um... yes," said Vicars, blinking at us through his glasses. "Oh. I don't know, maybe the end of March last," Vicars said. "Mr. Burtchaell asked if I could show the diamonds to his lady friend. Then early in June, I showed the diamonds to Mr. J.C. Hodgson, librarian to the Duke of Northumberland. From then, I have no recollection of seeing the jewels, nor of having gone to the safe."

Ross stared at him. "The Crown Jewels had not been checked in—over a month?"

"That's no problem," Vicars answered. "I was assured they were safe."

"That's bollocks," Ross snapped. "Weren't you aware that Mrs. O'Farrell reported she found the Office of Arms door opened on Wednesday, the 3rd of July?"

Ross waited for his words to sink in.

"Yes, of course. I thought that was of no consequence," Vicars said. "To the best of my recollection, Stivey informed me that he was told by the office cleaner that she found the hall door open when she arrived to clean the office in the morning. I told him it must be O'Keefe, the man responsible for the light in Bedford Tower."

"I call your attention to another occasion," Ross added. "Just over a month before the robbery, you were aware of the disappearance of the key to the safe, which was found by the same cleaning woman attached to a keyring with multiple other keys."

Vicars sighed. "Looking back, there is some fragment of truth to what she said." He excused his omission by claiming that the plans for the upcoming royal visit had swamped him with work. Being the resident expert on formal procedure, Lord Aberdeen relied heavily on him to plan the ceremonies for the King. Because of all these pressing concerns, Vicars claimed that the incident of the unlocked door had just slipped his mind.

The questioning continued for another half an hour until John Ross steeled himself, realizing we were achieving little. And we left.

JOURNAL #4—THE SAFE

09 July 1907

AT NINE O'CLOCK YESTERDAY, Sir John Ross emerged from his office and barked, "Where is everyone? I want your attention."

The detectives stopped chattering; all heads turned toward him. "Right, lads," he said into the silence. "You have no doubt heard of the robbery next door." He drew a deep breath before looking at his men. "The Office of Arms is only fifty yards away from our police station—no leads, no guards saw anything, no witness heard anything. This break-in makes the Metropolitan Police look inept. We were charged with providing nightly inspection to Dublin Castle."

Heads solemnly nodded.

The police commissioner said, "To make things worse, the King is arriving in three days. There's going to be hell to pay if we've come up with nothing. You were chosen because I felt you were the best detectives in Ireland."

A long silence.

"This is the worst theft in Irish history—the Irish Crown Jewels. Here's what we need to do," Ross told us. "And we need to do it right feckin' now. I've appointed Owen Kerr to be chief detective on this case because he was personally involved with the robbery on Friday night.

"Sergeant Kerr's opinion is the robbery was someone connected with the Office of Arms—an inside job. As of now, I'm inclined to agree. I told Kerr to assemble a list of possible suspects connected to the Office of Arms. There are nine of them. One is Sir Arthur Vicars. I will interview the Ulster King of Arms myself."

Ross told me to name the suspected persons.

"The three heralds," I said, "Francis Goldney, Francis Shackleton, and Pierce Gun Mahoney. Then we have Mary O'Farrell, the cleaning woman."

I checked my notes and added, "George Burtchaell, the Office of Arms Secretary; Phillips, Vicar's coachman; and O'Keefe, the man who lights the Tower clock at night."

Ross told me, "See Mary O'Farrell. Make certain the woman has a very, very poor memory." Ross turned to Detectives O'Hanlon and Conley. "You men check the three heralds: Goldney, Shackleton, and Mahoney. Find out where they were on Friday night—and if possible, confirm their statements.

"Detectives McKay and Kelly," Ross added, "your assignments will be Burtchaell, Phillips, and John O'Keefe. And I want you to know, I need this information by our five o'clock meeting. Sir David Harrel, the assistant superintendent, will be here. He'll want to hear what the best police in Ireland have to offer."

John Ross concluded, "I told you the king is coming to Dublin in three days. We need to make serious progress, or Lord Aberdeen will ask for assist from the English connection." Ross mumbled, "That means Scotland Yard."

*   *   *

LATER THAT MORNING, the two lock and safe experts arrived. The first was Mr. O'Hare of Milner's Safe Company. He had come to examine the lock on the strongroom door. For an hour, I watched O'Hare detaching the lock and examining it. He asked me, "Had the lock been picked, or had it been opened with a key?"

I said that I didn't know.

O'Hare told me that the lock could not have been picked. He said, "The lock, an expensive one, has a shiny scratch-free surface. Any attempt to pick the lock would have left crude scratches. The lock must have been opened with a key. It could not be opened from a wax impression. A wax impression would have left some trace."

The lock on the safe in the library was examined in the same way by Cornelius Gallagher. He spent two-and-a-half hours examining the Ratner lock as meticulously as O'Hare had checked the Milner on the strongroom door. He pointed out to me the unblemished surface and insisted this also ruled out a wax impression. "Whoever opened the lock, "he said, "did so with his own key."

*   *   *

AT THREE O'CLOCK, I WENT to Mrs. O'Farrell's house. A deep sadness crept over me as I related what Ross had made me say. "If you want to keep your job at Dublin Castle, you never, ever have seen Lord Haddo in the Office of Arms."

With a glance of mingled contempt, Mary O'Farrell nodded. "Yes."

Sir David Harrel was in attendance along with the detectives at Commissioner Ross's five p.m. meeting. "Tell us about the safe experts, Kerr," Ross said to me.

I explained that regarding the safe and the strongroom door, both experts had examined them carefully and concluded there were no wax impressions. "Whoever opened the safe, they said, had done so with their own key."

Sir David Harrel gave me an annoyed look.

Ross said, "Report on Stivey and the cleaning woman."

I said that I had ruled out Mrs. Mary O'Farrell and William Stivey, because neither of them had access to the keys, except for Stivey on Saturday, when Vicars had asked him to put a collar in the safe and he discovered the theft.

"How about the heralds?" Ross asked Detective Conley.

"Most of them were not in Dublin on the night of the robbery, sir," he said. "Dublin Herald Francis Shackleton was in England on the 8th of July."

Conley paused. "Shackleton was also a guest of the Duke of Argyll. I fear his alibi is watertight for the period of the robbery. It would be embarrassing to confirm it with His Majesty's brother-in-law.

"It's also worth noting, sir," Conley continued, "that Shackleton shares a house with Sir Arthur Vicars, so he may have had access to the key, as did Mr. Pierce Gun Mahoney, who we were informed visited Sir Arthur's house regularly."

Conley checked his notes. He added, "I do not suspect Francis Goldney. He had no opportunity to access the safe, and he was only in Dublin three days in May."

"Who interrogated Pierce Gun Mahoney?" Ross inquired.

Detective O'Hanlon said, "I handled that interview. Pierce Gun Mahoney told me that he had the strongroom key from his uncle, Sir Arthur Vicars."

Ross asked, "Did Sir Arthur ever discuss with you the correctness of his being allowed to keep the key?"

"He said his uncle considered that as he was Cork Herald, he should have the key. I asked him, did he come into the Office of Arms on the 6th of July?

"He answered, yes, he was there in the morning, between eleven and twelve. I asked, how late? Mr. Mahoney said that he left when the office staff left."

O'Hanlon said, "I confirmed with his household staff: Mr. Pierce Gun Mahoney had dinner with his family and never left home that Friday night."

"I guess it's my turn," Detective McKay said. "Kelly and I handled Burtchaell, John O'Keefe, and Vicar's coachman, Phillips.

"What we found was that John O'Keefe, the Board of Works official responsible for the light in Bedford Tower's clock, professes he never knew of the existence of the Crown Jewels before their disappearance. Kelly and I both believe him. Next, we questioned George Burtchaell, the Office of Arms Secretary. He tried to protect his boss, Sir Arthur Vicars. I pressed him, 'Mr. Burtchaell, the room we are now sitting in is the library?'

"'Yes,' he said.

"'Can you see the safe?'

"George Burtchaell nodded that he could see the safe.

"I asked him, 'Is that the safe in which the Crown Jewels were deposited?' When he said yes, I asked him, during office hours, was the door to the Office of Arms locked or not? Burtchaell was forced to admit it was not locked. Which meant that anyone could enter. Then I asked about the keys to the strongroom. He admitted he was unsure of the number of keys. Vicars and Stivey each had one. He said he had a third, which was now in a drawer in the strongroom, and Mr. Mahoney also had one. I asked him why.

"Burtchaell said Mr. Mahoney was a volunteer, and as Cork Herald, an unpaid officer, would only come to the office on certain occasions. Sir, I believe Burtchaell never had a key to the safe, and as such, is not a suspect."

O'Hanlon finished his list with Vicars's coachman. "Phillips was turned inside out by our investigation. He's an honest, hard-working man, and to add to his woes, Vicars dismissed him."

"That leaves Sir Arthur Vicars," Ross said, trying to contain his irritation. "When I tried to make an appointment, he said, 'Is it really necessary? I've got so much to do before the king's arrival.'

"I told him it was really *very* necessary." Ross closed his eyes and shook his head. He mumbled, "That ninny."

7

JOURNAL #5—THE KING'S ARRIVAL

11 July 1907

YESTERDAY, ON THURSDAY, the day King Edward VII visited Ireland, I was assigned to be one of the crowd-control officers when the royal party disembarked from His Majesty's ship, the *Victoria and Albert*, in Kingstown. Commissioner John Ross had advised us, "Be aware, there might be demonstrations of opposition. Groups like Sinn Féin and other Irish nationalists might be organizing protests."

I had seen no signs of any protest. Residents of Kingstown had prepared for the royal visit by decorating their homes. Festoons of laurels decked the Town Hall from top to bottom. Mottoes of "God bless our King" in crimson and gold were draped over the balconies of the large-terraced houses and small hotels along the route.

By ten o'clock, crowds had begun to congregate. When Lord Lieutenant Aberdeen, dressed in his military uniform, arrived, he received a huge welcome.

When their majesties came ashore, I was stationed near the dock. In attendance were the Irish nobility, many of whom were Knights of the Order of St. Patrick.

The King, brown-haired, neatly bearded and mustached, wore a morning dress and top-hat, and, I guess to honor the Irish linen industry, he had donned a green poplin tie. Her Majesty, the Queen, wore a black-and-white dress with a light grey wrap. A few paces back, the Naval Band played the National Anthem, and the guard of honor gave the royal salute. Lord Aberdeen escorted their majesties to the royal carriage to begin the five-mile trip to Ballsbridge, where King Edward was scheduled to tour the Irish International Exhibition.

Shortly after half past seven, the first day of the royal visit came to an end. Thousands of holidaymakers and sightseers still crammed the seafront and promenade at Kingstown. The gathering dusk of the fine summer evening was illuminated by tiny lanterns being lit on the royal yachts lying at anchor in the calm waters of the harbor. Then, with a whoosh and a crack like thunder, the fireworks display began. Rockets trailed their orange wake into the night sky, bursting to send hundreds of green, red and yellow balls of smoking fire dropping gently back into the sea.

8

JOURNAL #6—SCOTLAND YARD INSPECTOR

12 July 1907

ON FRIDAY MORNING, SIR JOHN ROSS told me that he had received word from Ireland's Chief Secretary, Augustine Birrell, that King Edward VII was, understandably, less than impressed with our Dublin Metropolitan Police results.

Birrell told Ross that he was present when the King said that the theft of the Crown Jewels was a political embarrassment for him because Dublin Castle was the British administration's base in Ireland, and he felt the lost jewels were seen as symbolic of his inability to reign.

"Sir, everything that can be done is being done," Birrell said he told the King. "We posted a reward of 1,000 pounds in return for any information aiding in the return of the jewels, and Scotland Yard has sent one of their best detectives to find the person responsible for the theft."

John Ross paused in his explanation because a man of medium height, balding and slim, had entered the police station.

"My name is John Kane," he said. "I'm a chief inspector from Scotland Yard. I met with your superintendent, Sir John Lowe, early this morning, and he suggested that I should meet with you, Commissioner." Kane looked like a man with an air of experience.

Ross had told me early on that all men from Scotland Yard were glory-seeking smart alecks. I could tell the man from

London sensed a wariness in Commissioner Ross as soon as they shook hands.

"It's very good of you to come over, Mr. Kane," said Sir John. "I only hope it's going to be worthwhile. This is Sergeant Owen Kerr, chief detective on this case. I presume you'll want to know how we're getting on with the jewel theft?"

"It would be a help, sir," replied Kane. "I wouldn't want to duplicate your efforts. I'm sure you'll have covered all the ground."

Ross gave a brief, bitter smile. "Not all the ground. My concern is how a thief could enter the Office of Arms. The man would have had to walk into the Bedford Tower portico in plain view of the guarding constable. At night, nobody had any business going into the offices, except Detective Sergeant Owen Kerr when he made his nightly rounds."

Kane asked me, "Did you question the night constable?"

I said the constable had seen nothing unusual, and he reported that nobody had entered the offices while he patrolled the Upper Castle Yard.

"Obviously, someone had." Kane shrugged. "So we must find out who."

"Do you have other Scotland Yard detectives with you?" Ross asked.

"No, I'm alone. If it wouldn't be too much trouble, may I avail myself of your sergeant here? He could fill me in on the details of the case and be a notetaker for my investigation. As you know, suspects say things—and later deny them."

As they stared at each other, Ross said, "Are you okay with this, Kerr?"

I said, "I think at this point, sir, I should talk to you privately."

John Kane excused himself.

"We've gotten nowhere on this robbery," I said to Ross. "I believe with full co-operation between the Dublin Metropolitan Police and the inspector from Scotland Yard, we may clear up this robbery. You will share the credit. What's the harm?"

"Go on, then," Sir Ross said with a sigh. "Get on out there."

When I left Ross's office, Inspector Kane asked me, "Did he say yes?"

When I said yes, Kane asked me where the nearest pub was.

"The Sackville Café," I told him.

"Do they have a smoking room?"

"Indeed, they do."

*   *   *

THE SACKVILLE CAFÉ, LIKE MOST common drinking establishments in Dublin, had a simple, cozy interior with wooden floors, dim overhead lighting, pictures on the walls of Irish musicians and sports teams, and in winter, a welcoming fireplace. They had a limited drink menu with a strong focus on ales and stouts. We ordered two Guinnesses.

Chief Inspector Kane tamped some Navy-cut tobacco into his briar pipe and lit it. "Well, Sergeant," he groused. "Did Commissioner John Ross give you permission to accompany me—and be his *spy?*"

"Yes," I replied. "Of course. When you go back to London, my boss will still be Sir John Ross. Plus, the theft of the jewels was on my watch. Superintendent John Lowe and David Harrel feel that I may have been responsible. If I can be a partner in locating the jewels or the thieves, it will allay their doubts."

He held me with his eyes. Staring. "Can I trust you, Sergeant?"

"As much as I can trust you, Inspector."

A puff of laughter burst out. "Good answer." He quietly sipped his beer. "I was born in Ireland, Listowel, County Kerry—"

"Inspector Kane," I interrupted. "If Scotland Yard was aware of the robbery five days ago, why did you just arrive today?"

"Impressive, mate," Kane told me. "Nothing escapes you." He seemed to dither before he spoke. "I had other responsibilities, and it would also have been inappropriate for me to start an investigation while the King was in Ireland."

I knew that chief inspector John Kane was lying to me. I fell silent. He gave me an inscrutable smile and changed the subject. "It's been a while since I'm back. This morning, I stepped off the mail boat at Kingstown and took the Dublin train; went to meet Superintendent Sir John Lowe. He told me, 'You have to be very circumspect in your investigation, because the motive for the robbery might be political.'"

"Could you explain that?" I asked.

"The political relationship between Ireland and Great Britain is troubled, with a rising tide of Irish nationalism. It's possible some nationalists might have stolen the jewels just to embarrass the King and Lord Aberdeen."

"Yeah," I said. "That might be."

"Well, let's not mince words," Kane told me. "Let's start at the beginning. Friday night, the fifth of July, what time did you make your inspections?"

"Soon after seven o'clock."

"Did you observe anyone present in any single office?"

"No," I told him. "The blinds were drawn, and I saw no one present."

"It was dark at night," Kane said. "If the blinds were drawn, but lights were on in the Office of Arms, wouldn't the guards have noticed?"

I said, "I can't answer that."

Kane hinted, "Someone may have used a pocket-sized carbon filament bulb. Apparently, they knew the layout of the safe. When you made your inspection, what time did you come into the room with the safe?"

"The safe was in the library. It was the first room I entered."

"Why placed in the library?" Kane asked.

I tried to explain. "A few years ago, the Chairman of the Board of Works decided that a strongroom needed to be built in Bedford Tower to house valuable objects in a secure safe. But when the work was completed, it was found that the door of the strongroom was too low and too narrow to admit the safe. As far as I heard, despite the offer of the chairman to remedy this situation, Vicars declined his offer, and then the safe was placed in the library."

"What's in the strongroom?" Kane said.

"Three collars and badges belonging to the Knights of St. Patrick, as well as two silver state maces, plus the Irish Sword of State, a jeweled scepter, and other valuables."

"Who had all the various keys?"

I said, "The staff of Vicars's office; Mary O'Farrell, the cleaning woman; myself; and John O'Keefe had keys to the door of the Office of Arms. The only two keys to the safe in the library were held by Sir Arthur Vicars. There were also four keys to the strongroom, held by Vicars; Stivey; Vicars's nephew, Pierce Gun Mahoney; and George Burtchaell, Vicars's secretary."

"Could there have been a wax impress of any keys?"

"No. The manufacturers of both the safe and the strongroom locks carefully inspected the locks. I was there. They told me both the safe and strongroom locks were found not to have been forced, and no duplicate keys had been used."

Kane nodded. "What do you think of Vicars?"

"I've had ample opportunity to study Sir Arthur, and I rather like what I've seen. He is a fussy man; a man who cares for small details rather than reality. I sense Vicars as having integrity, devoid of cunning, but also a man of great naïveté."

John Kane gave a vague smile. He checked his watch. "Where is he now?"

"Vicars usually arrives before noon on Friday," I said. "I expect he will be in his Office of Arms in Bedford Tower."

"The adage about turning over a stone and waiting to see what crawls out from underneath has great relevance in this case," Kane said. "This investigation now enters its murky phase. Let's go visit the Ulster King of Arms."

*   *   *

WE MET SIR ARTHUR VICARS in his office in the Office of Arms in Belford Towers. Kane introduced himself, saying, "My name is Chief Inspector John Kane from Scotland Yard. I think you know Sergeant Kerr."

"That's a reasonable assumption," Vicars said. "The man was on duty when—"

Kane broke in, "Sir Arthur, Lord Aberdeen has requested Scotland Yard to help solve the Crown Jewels robbery. Would it be in order to put a few questions to you?"

"Of course, my dear chap. Anything you want to know, just inquire."

"Sir, there was no forced entry," Kane told him. "In spite of the overwhelming evidence of an inside job, you continue to voice your opinion that no member of the staff of your Office of Arms could have committed the robbery."

Vicars was taken aback by what John Kane was saying. He stonewalled. "I have implicit confidence in every member of my staff," he insisted.

The three of us went down to the library and viewed the scene of the crime.

Kane asked Vicars to offer his own theory of the theft. Flying in the face of the known facts, Vicars suggested that someone had gotten a wax impression of his keys and had stolen the jewels.

Kane reminded Sir Arthur of the opinion of the two locksmiths, that there had been no wax impression.

Vicars fumbled for an answer.

The Scotland Yard inspector had done his homework well. He asked Vicars to explain to him about the ribbon left behind. Vicars explained, "A piece of silk ribbon attached to the Star was carefully detached and replaced in the box."

"A normal thief could simply yank the badge out," Kane said. "Who cares about a silk ribbon when you're stealing a jeweled badge worth a fortune? Experience has taught me that the first thing uppermost in the thief's mind is to secure his retreat. He wants to get away. To my mind," he continued, "the man who did that has a knowledge of this building and was not rushed."

Kane's message was clear. "The theft quite plainly was not 'in another person's house' but on familiar ground." He bluntly stated, "There were two keys to the safe that were in your possession, Sir Arthur."

"Yes. One around my neck and another hidden in my bedroom."

Kane continued, "There are four keys to the lock on the strongroom door, held by yourself; William Stivey; your secretary, George Burtchaell; and your nephew, Pierce Gun Mahoney." His grey eyes steady, he asked Vicars to explain why his nephew had a key.

Vicars had a nervous smile. "Mr. Mahoney is a volunteer, and as Cork Herald, an unpaid officer, and I thought he should have the strongroom key."

Kane checked his notes. "Did the other two heralds, Shackleton and Goldney, have keys?"

"No."

I interrupted. "I need a word with you, Mr. Kane."

We stepped out into the hallway. I told Kane, "Our police investigation has revealed that Mr. Shackleton is co-tenant with Sir Arthur at 7 St. James's Terrace, and Mr. Pierce Gun Mahoney visited Sir Arthur's house regularly."

He nodded. "Yes, I know that."

When we returned, Kane asked Vicars, trying to avoid a patronizing tone, "Does Mr. Shackleton live in your home, sir?"

Sir Arthur snorted. "Yes. Mr. Shackleton lives in England. He only comes to Dublin on occasion; that's why I share my house with him—and he pays rent."

"Can I ask you, sir, if you know Captain Richard Gorges?"

A frown flitted across Sir Arthur's face. "I know Gorges," he said. "He's a friend of Shackleton's from the South African War. To be frank, Chief Inspector, he's not one of my favorite acquaintances. I've had occasions to warn Shackleton about him."

"Why, sir?"

"Oh, nothing in particular," said Sir Arthur hurriedly. "I just don't think he's a very good influence. Bit of a wild man, don't you know."

"A wild man?" Kane asked.

Vicars refused to be drawn out any longer on the subject. He checked his watch. "I think that's all the time I have for you," he said, and walked out of the library.

After he left, Kane said to me, "When you make the report to your commissioner, tell him the robbery wasn't on Friday night. It was a few days earlier."

"That's crazy," I said. "One copper to another. What's your opinion?"

John Kane answered, "I'm convinced that the jewels were deliberately stolen in advance of the royal visit, so all alibis are useless. There were insiders."

He smiled and said, "Tomorrow, we need to speak to the three heralds. Goodnight, mate."

9

JOURNAL #7—HARK THE HERALDS

13 July 1907

INSPECTOR JOHN KANE AND I INTERVIEWED Pierce Gun Mahoney in the library of the Office of Arms. I took notes. Mahoney affirmed he was given both a latchkey for the outer door of the office and a strongroom key when his uncle was away, but he had not returned them when Sir Arthur came back from vacation in December 1906.

"What was the need of your having the strongroom key?" Kane inquired.

"When I came in here, you see, in the morning, I could unlock the strongroom door, if nobody else was in, and let me get out the books."

"Books?" Kane asked.

Mahoney said, "My position as Cork Herald involved granting and confirming coats of arms, maintaining genealogical records, and overseeing matters of heraldry, so I needed the key."

Kane wasn't buying that one. "But Stivey had a key, you know!"

"Yes, but sometimes he's not in," Mahoney lamely said.

I added, "But it was William Stivey's habit to be here at ten."

"Yes. I suppose so."

"For what purpose," said Kane, ignoring Mahoney's tone of injured innocence, "could the strongroom door be opened before eleven in the morning?"

"None that I know of," admitted Mahoney.

Then Kane asked, "Can you suggest why you should have been allowed a key to the strongroom after Sir Arthur Vicars returned to Dublin? And did your uncle ever discuss with you the propriety of your being allowed to keep it?"

"Well, I think he considered me having the key because I am the Cork Herald."

Kane ignore his answer. "Did you often visit Sir Arthur's home?"

"Of course; he is my uncle."

"On what occasions?"

"Some gatherings."

"While you were at *some* gatherings, was Mr. Shackleton there?"

"Yes. Francis was a co-tenant with Sir Arthur at 7 St. James's Terrace."

"Who else was at the gatherings?" Kane continued.

"Shackleton's friend from the war, Richard Gorges, and Lord Haddo."

"Lord Aberdeen's eldest son?"

"That's correct," Mahoney said.

"Was Mr. Francis Goldney there?"

"No. Goldney only stayed with Sir Arthur in May during the opening of the International Exhibition."

"Anyone else?"

Pierce Gun Mahoney hesitated before answering. He spoke in a confiding whisper. "John Campbell, the Duke of Argyll."

John Kane had a worried look. He shrugged. "That's it for now. I appreciate your honesty, Mr. Mahoney."

When Mahoney left, Kane told me that John Campbell, the Duke of Argyll, was married to Her Royal Highness

Princess Louise Caroline Alberta, fourth daughter of Queen Victoria, and the King's brother-in-law.

*   *   *

FRANCIS BENNETT GOLDNEY ALSO MET US in the library. When Kane questioned him, Goldney said he lived almost full-time in England and was Mayor of Canterbury.

He also advised us he held the office of Athlone Pursuiant in the Office of Arms, Dublin Castle. Following his appointment by Lord Aberdeen in May 1907, he stayed for three or four days as a guest of Sir Arthur Vicars for the opening ceremony for the International Exhibition in Ballsbridge.

"When did you arrive in Dublin this time?" Kane asked.

"My intention had been to arrive in Dublin shortly before the King's visit on the 10th of July, but when I received Vicars's telegram, I quickly changed my plans an got on a boat the night of the 7th and disembarked from the mailboat at seven o'clock on the morning of Monday the 8th, in wretched condition." Goldney sighed. "The crossing had been a rough one."

John Kane agreed, "My crossing was pretty much the same, but Scotland Yard sent me here to try and resolve the Crown Jewel robbery. So may I ask you some questions?"

Goldney emitted a brief, ragged sigh, "Please do that."

"You said that you only stayed in Dublin for three days at the opening of the exhibition, and you stayed with Sir Arthur Vicars. Correct?"

He nodded.

"Were there any conversations about the jewels that you can remember?"

"Yes. I saw the jewels on that occasion in May."

"Please tell us how."

"Well, I accompanied Lady Donegall and Lady Orford, and another lady, an American, a friend of Lady Donegall's. Sir Arthur asked them if they would like to see the State Rooms and other things in the castle, and then we went over to the State Rooms, and when we came back to the library, Sir Arthur showed us the jewels."

"Did Sir Arthur volunteer to show them the jewels?"

Goldney said, "Whether anyone asked to see the jewels or not, I do not know. I remember Lady Orford saying she thought it was a great pity that the jewels should be shut up in a place like this in the library. Sir Arthur patted the safe. He said, 'This one was built by the Ratner Safe Company, and it was built to keep the jewels safe.'"

"Did you ever see the jewels again?" Kane questioned.

"No. But I heard from Mahoney about what Lord Haddo did."

"Can you tell us about it?"

"Vicars," Goldney said, "was a lightweight drinker. The parties at Bedford Tower weren't orgies, but rather wholesome pranks. At one of these parties, Mahoney told me, 'Vicars got so drunk that he passed out in his office. His drinking buddies got themselves an idea. It was a prank, not a theft.'

"I was told Lord Haddo rifled through Vicars's clothes and found keys to the safe. Then he went downstairs to the library, opened the safe, took out the Irish Crown Jewels, tiptoed back upstairs, and replaced the keys where he had found them."

Goldney added, "I'm sure Vicars got quite a surprise a few days later, when he received a package containing the jewels. This might explain why, after the real theft, Vicars maintained that it was all no big deal, and that the jewels would just show up."

Without John Kane asking him, Goldney said, "If you think I was party to the recent theft, you're wrong. I had no keys to the Office of Arms or the safe or the strongroom, and before the robbery, I was in England."

Kane thanked him for the information.

When Francis Goldney had left, Kane mused aloud, "Sir Arthur's limited capacity for drink was well known. With the key to the safe in his pocket, the guardian of the Crown Jewels goes to sleep."

He breathed a deep sigh.

*　　*　　*

FRANCIS SHACKLETON WAS THE LAST herald we interviewed that day. He informed us that he'd first become connected with this office in about October 1899, when he was appointed Assistant Secretary to the Office of Arms by Sir Arthur Vicars. From May 1900, he was living in barracks in Dublin as an officer in the 3rd Battalion Royal Irish Fusiliers, Armagh Militia. On being invalided out in September 1901, he moved to Devonshire, England.

"When did you come back to Dublin?" Kane asked.

Shackleton said he could not remember when he'd first come back to Dublin, but knew he was there for the King's visit in 1903.

Kane said, "Can you tell us at what date you took up your residence in St. James's Terrace with Sir Arthur Vicars?"

"I think in July 1905."

"What was the arrangement between you and Arthur Vicars?"

"The arrangement between Vicars and myself was this: I paid half the rent rates and taxes, half the servants' wages, board and ordinary wages. And I paid for half of all the repairs in the house."

"That seems to have been a very favorable arrangement for Sir Arthur Vicars," Kane remarked. "You say you occupied the place for about two months a year?"

"That is about right."

Kane pressed, "While you were living in the house, you were well acquainted with Sir Arthur Vicars's habits?"

"Yes, of course, I was well acquainted with them."

"Did Vicars ever give you a key for the door of the Office of Arms?"

"No."

"Or the key of the strongroom or the safe?"

"God's truth, never," Shackleton said.

"How often would you come to the office while you were residing in Dublin?"

Shackleton answered, "Pretty much every day."

"Had you ever had occasion to go to the strongroom?"

"Frequently. The strongroom was opened all day by Stivey, the office messenger."

John Kane checked his notes again. "I am going to ask you some questions. You need not answer them unless you like. Have you had monetary difficulties?"

Shackleton took a deep breath. "Yes," he said. "My difficulties could easily have been relieved had I chosen to go to my family and tell them; but for various reasons I did not care to do so, and I borrowed money, not from my banker, but from a moneylender. You may ask any question you like, but I understood my coming here was merely in relation to theft of the jewels. But I am quite prepared to answer any of your questions."

Kane asked, "Where were you when you learned about the robbery?"

"I was in Penshurst in Kent for the weekend," he said. "Lord Ronald Sutherland Gowe first saw it in the paper and called my attention to it. The Duke of Argyll was there also. I felt I should be in Dublin and changed my plans. I crossed on the evening of the 8th and arrived in the morning and went to Arthur Vicars's house at Clonskeagh."

"Did you, on that morning," Kane said, "discuss with Sir Arthur Vicars as to how the robbery could have occurred?"

Shackleton seemed confused. "I am not quite sure that I did. Not to any extent that I can remember. Sir Arthur seemed quite overwhelmed by the whole thing."

Kane asked, "Do you have any information that would throw light on the theft of these jewels? Can you assist us?"

"Not in any way," Shackleton said. "I have absolutely no knowledge. I cannot even suggest a possible solution—"

Kane interrupted, "Have you ever seen the jewels?"

"Oh, yes. I saw Sir Arthur Vicars taking them out and showing them. The last time, I think, to my recollection, was Horse Show week of 1906. Vicars showed them to Lady Orford and Lady Donegall, who were here at that time."

Kane continued, "Any other time?"

Shackleton seemed confused. That was Kane's intention.

He shrugged. "I know perfectly well that I was accused of aiding Lord Haddo in stealing the keys, opening the safe, and displaying the Crown Jewels while Sir Arthur had been drinking too much and was asleep upstairs in the Office of Arms. But I had no part in that charade. It was irresponsible, and Lord Haddo returned them the next day."

"I believe you," Kane admitted. He turned the next page over in his notes. "When we spoke with Sir Arthur, he was not happy with your friend Richard Gorges. He said he warned you about him."

He laughed mirthlessly. "No, that was not uncommon. They are very different. Sir Arthur can be a very proper, fussy person, but Richard Gorges emerged from the Boer War a much-decorated man, awarded a Queen's Medal with five clasps and a King's Medal with two clasps."

"Impressive," Kane acknowledged.

Shackleton added, "My friendship with Richard Gorges goes back to 1901 in Cape Town. I was a lieutenant in the 3rd Battalion of the Royal Irish Fusiliers, and Gorges was a captain in the Royal Lancaster Regiment. I was wounded; a blasted Boer sniper got me just above my right elbow. The doctor thought it smashed up my muscle a bit, and the Army sent me home to be discharged."

"What happened to your *friend?*" Kane asked.

"After the Boer War, Gorges was posted to Border Security in South Africa, then back to England. He was appointed a captain, and the Regimental Musketry Instructor. Gorges divided his time between Portsmouth and Ireland."

Shackleton's questioning had lasted for nearly one hour, far longer than that of Pierce Gun Mahoney or Francis Goldney. I could see this incredibly charming man, handsome and clever, had won over John Kane.

But not me. The man was a professional liar.

10

JOURNAL #8—CHAIN OF COMMAND

13 July 1907

COMISSIONER ROSS SUMMONED John Kane into his office. I followed. "Inspector Kane," Ross said. "You've been investigating the theft situation for several days. What have you to report?"

Kane hesitated. "About the Crown Jewels—"

"Of course," interrupted Sir John impatiently. "His Majesty is very interested in the outcome. They're his bloody jewels."

"Quite so, Sir John," Kane said. "We need to be cautious in the investigations."

"Go on." He seemed impatient with Kane's meandering answer.

"Well, sir, to be blunt, Commissioner, I must inform you that our investigations have uncovered quite a nest of vipers in Dublin Castle."

An alarmed expression flitted across Sir John's face. "Vipers?" he said. "A nest of vipers, Mr. Kane?"

Kane answered, "We have evidence that Sir Arthur Vicars entertained men known to us as sexual deviants at his home at Clonskeagh, and that at these parties, abominable acts took place between various guests, including Mr. Shackleton, who shares the home with Sir Arthur, as you'll know."

"Good God!" cried Sir John. "Are you sure?"

"At these *parties*," Kane answered, "the Cork Herald, Mr. Pierce Mahoney, and a captain in the Army by the name of Richard Gorges were also present." He hesitated. "Lord

Haddo made a habit of attending these functions. I personally took a statement from a gentleman in London, Peter McEnnery, who participated in these unnatural acts, and we are certain of our evidence."

The commissioner clasped both hands to his forehead and then pulled them back through his grey hair. "This is terrible news, Mr. Kane," he said quietly. He was silent for more than a minute, looking down at his blotter, the enormity of the situation permeating slowly into his mind. "This is terrible," Ross repeated.

"Yes, sir," Kane responded. "Particularly since one part of the alibi of Shackleton concerning the Crown Jewel robbery is that he was spending the weekend in England in the company of His Majesty's brother-in-law."

Sir John was quiet. He seemed still unable to grasp fully the awful implications of what Kane had told him. After his silence, he raised his head slowly and looked directly into Kane's eyes. "You said, Mr. Kane, that you have reports of observations?"

"From officers from Scotland Yard," Kane said.

"On whose orders?" demanded Sir John, his voice rising. "On whose orders, Chief Inspector, since this information was not known to me?"

"On the orders of the Commissioner of the London Metropolitan Police, sir," said Kane, unaware of the anger that was about to break over him.

"He had no right to send men to Dublin without my permission," Ross growled. "Did your London Commissioner take it into his head to send men here—in secret?"

"I believe not, sir," said Kane. He paused, straightening in his chair and slipping his pipe into his coat pocket.

"Stop prevaricating, man," exclaimed Sir John, rising from his chair and stalking round his desk to loom over Kane. His face was white with anger. "Just tell me all you know, Chief Inspector."

"It's not really my place to do so, sir. I merely carry out my orders."

"Chief Inspector," Ross said, "unless I see that report, I shall order you from Dublin at this instant."

"Sir, from my knowledge the Commissioner of the London Metropolitan Police was acting under direct orders from the Home Office and the Home Secretary. This was felt to be an investigation that should be handled in the most confidential manner."

Sir John Ross stared down at Kane for a moment, turned away abruptly, and walked back to his desk. He sat down and pulled his writing pad towards him. "I am communicating immediately with Mr. Gladstone, the Home Secretary, to protest at this secretive inquiry by Scotland Yard. I shall also mention that, in my opinion, you are being less than frank with me even now. Have you never heard of the chain of command?"

Kane began to protest, but the Chief Commissioner continued, "I shall demand that this inquiry be left entirely to the Dublin Police force and the Royal Irish Constabulary as far as investigations in Ireland are concerned. Is that clear, Chief Inspector?"

"Yes, sir."

"You may leave."

"Sir, before I do," Kane continued. "May I say how much I regret the stance you have chosen to adopt."

Ross snapped, "You may do as you wish, Chief Inspector. Sergeant Kerr will continue his investigation under my orders and at my direction. Clear?"

"Sir," replied Kane flatly. He began moving towards the door.

"And, Chief Inspector," Sir John called just as Kane was opening the door. "I wouldn't plan on your stay in Dublin being any longer than it takes for the Home Secretary to reply to my letter."

Kane turned back towards the desk, thought better of it, and merely replied again, "Sir."

I could see that something had gone seriously wrong.

11

JOURNAL #9—JOHN KANE'S REPORT

17 July 1907

LAST NIGHT WAS MY FINAL MEETING with Chief Inspector John Kane. We met in the lounge bar of the Clarence Hotel on Essex Street East, where Kane was staying.

He shook his head. "Owen," Kane said quietly. "I submitted my report to Commissioner Ross, to Superintendent Lowe, and also to the Irish Secretary, Augustine Birrell.

"This morning, I was summoned by Ross to Dublin Castle. Birrell must have shared my report with Lord Aberdeen. As a result, Lord Aberdeen advised Ross my mission to Dublin was completed and I should return to London immediately."

I asked, "What about the Crown Jewels robbery?"

Kane shrugged. "I could have solved that theft, were it not for the royal involvement. I listed the circumstances of the robbery, and I expounded my theory that the theft bore all the hallmarks of an inside job. I then exposed Sir Arthur's homosexual court and its ties to Lord Gower's circle in London."

"Did you discuss Lord Haddo?"

"No. I had a hunch but wanted to meet with him once again. Why did you ask?"

"He's a good fella," I told Kane. "On one occasion Haddo took the Insignia as a practical joke. I doubt he would have repeated the exercise. When Haddo removed the jewels as a prank, he became a marked man. We were aware of what had happened, and I don't think he wanted to take the extra risk for personal gain."

"That may be partially true," Kane said with a taut smile.

I told him that I was very sorry that he was leaving, but since Ross wanted me to now oversee the investigation, I needed to ask his advice.

"Go ahead, mate," he said.

"I'm confused. I don't understand why you tried to shield Francis Shackleton from your inquiry?"

Kane sighed and frowned at me, like a teacher addressing a student. "As for Mr. Shackleton, I fear his alibi is watertight for the period of the robbery, and it would be embarrassing to test it with his Majesty's brother-in-law included in it. I needed to fend off Shackleton about the homosexualism. Shackleton could put the 'Cat amongst the Pigeons' if he went to the press and exposed the King's brother-in-law. No mistake. The King would be furious. It would all fall on me, and my career."

I didn't know what to say, so I was silent.

He said, "A word of advice. Things will be different now. Be careful. When the iron glove falls, you don't want to be beneath it!"

12

JOURNAL #10—SIR JOHN ROSS

20 July 1907

AFTER JOHN KANE WENT BACK TO LONDON, Sir John Ross called me into his office. I was expecting to be transferred to petty theft or public drunkenness. Dublin was not considered a particularly dangerous or crime-ridden city.

Ross's office was small and dim, crowded with heavy chairs. He closed the door and gestured for me to take an empty chair. I was clearly nervous.

When we were seated, the commissioner stroked his grey beard and looked at me. He closed his eyes. "When I took this post, Sergeant Kerr, in 1902, it was with the expectation that I would be working with the legendary Inspector Michael Kerr, the greatest detective in the greatest police force in the world. Your father. You can imagine my dismay upon arriving in Dublin to find Mr. Kerr had already resigned. I suspect you share my dismay?"

I said, "Yes, sir."

"And so, I had missed my opportunity to work with him. Your father made his name over his tracking down of Charles Stewart Parnell and successfully bringing to book Joe Brady and Tim Kelly, who were directly involved in the Phoenix Park murders of 6 May 1882."

Ross added, "But then, I sent for you. Rather than pussy-foot around, I knew at that time you had little experience as a police officer, correct?"

"Well, sir," I told him. "I acted as constable for four years in Dún Laoghaire. I had no experience whatsoever as a detective."

Commissioner Ross waved my suggestion away like a bad odor. "That's not at all what I'm getting at, son. Maybe you have your father's genetic factor. I rely on my instincts, and that means that I trust you to be up to the job."

"What job?"

"Don't prove me wrong," Ross said. "We don't need Scotland Yard. I need *you* to find the goddamn jewels."

I said, "I'll do my very best, sir."

PART III

AFTERWARDS

...13

THE PATH

A LIGHT HIGHLAND DRIZZLE was falling on Thursday as Meghan sipped coffee and downed her soda bread muffin. She had almost fallen asleep in her chair poring over Detective Owen Kerr's journals. From what Meghan had read, no documentary evidence existed that identified the culprits of the greatest unsolved heist in Irish history. The perpetrators of the most intriguing and mysterious crime of early 20th century Ireland were safely in their graves.

She wanted to work out the answers. In addition to her *Irish Times* files, she paid the four pounds per month and subscribed to the *British Newspaper Archive*. This allowed her to search most British and Irish historical newspapers online. She found a report of the robbery in the *Evening Irish Times* on Monday, 08 July 1907.

JEWEL ROBBERY AT DUBLIN CASTLE

SPECIAL ANNOUNCEMENT

At 2:30 p.m. on 6 July, an official connected with the Office of Arms, Dublin, had occasion to put some articles into the safe in which the State Jewels belonging to the Order of St. Patrick had been kept; trying to unlock the door, he discovered that it had been previously unlocked and on testing the lever of the door, it opened.

The last time on which this safe is known to have been opened was on 11 June last, and the jewels were inspected and found to be correct, and there appeared to be doubt, but the door was locked when the inspection was over.

There was no mark on the safe to indicate any violence was used to open it, nor is there any indication to show that access to the building was obtained otherwise than by regular means.

Meghan also found in the documents that on 9 July, Dublin Police Superintendent John Lowe had sent a report on the robbery to the office of Augustine Birrell, the Chief Secretary of Ireland.

Inspectors Lowe's Report
Dublin Metropolitan Police, Date Stamp: No 4997
Superintendent's Office, G Division, Received 9.7.1907

SUBJECT: LARCENY OF STATE JEWELS FROM DUBLIN CASTLE

I beg to state that between 3 and 4pm on 6 July, a messenger from the Office of Arms came to me and intimated that Sir Arthur Vicars desired to see me. I at once proceeded to the office indicated, where Sir Arthur informed me that a "Burglary" had been committed on the premises and that a number of State jewels, the estimated value of which is something about £30,000, had been stolen from a safe in one of his offices. The Jewels in question belong to the Order of St. Patrick, and consist of a diamond star, worn by the Grand Master of the Order, a diamond badge also worn by the Grand Master of the Order, and five collars belonging to the Earl of Howth, the Marquess of Ormonde, the Earl of Cork, the Earl of Enniskillen, and the Earl of Mayo.

I attach a bill giving the best description available of these articles, which is being circulated to the principal centers in Great Britain and on the Continent. So far as has been ascertained, these articles were last seen on 11 June, when Sir Arthur Vicars exhibited them to a Mr. Hodgson of Alnwick, Northumberland.

The loss was discovered between 2 and 3pm on 6 July when W. Stivey, the office messenger, had been sent from Sir Arthur's office with a collar belonging to the Order to place it in the safe, of which he had been given the key.

A description of the missing jewels was wired to New Scotland Yard, London, with a request for special search and inquiry to be made regarding their disposal. Inquiries have been made from the Constables on duty in the vicinity of the Upper Castle Yard, but nothing of a suspicious nature appears to have come to their knowledge. I recommended to Chief Secretary Augustine Birrell to offer an award.

The matter is being pursued vigorously and any important information obtained will be at once reported.

Superintendent Lowe

Meghan wanted to work out the answers to her questions. From her crime reporting routine, she typed on her computer: *What, where and when did it happen*, and finally *how did it happen?* Now, she had a roadmap, a timeline—a path.

She reviewed her listing and decided to check where it had all begun—Dublin Castle.

...14

DUBLIN CASTLE

MEGHAN SECURED AN APPOINTMENT in the early afternoon with the curator, Dr. Bryce Hardy, at the Office of Arms section of Dublin Castle. She needed to find out more about the theft of the jewels.

There was still a light Highland drizzle when she left. The wind, freshened by daylight, was dispensing the fog, though it left the air damp and cold. Dublin was built for pedestrians and carriages, not for buses or cars; it's full of winding medieval streets, and when it rains the traffic goes into gridlock. Meghan took a cab down to Dublin Castle on Dame Street.

When she left the taxi, she took a moment to scan the castle with its fortified walls. Housed between its two main gates was the Bedford Tower, home of the Office of Arms. She snapped a photo of the tower.

She met Dr. Bryce Hardy in his office. The curator was a portly figure well into his mid-sixties, dressed in a thick tweed suit.

"I appreciate your being able to see me today in your Office of Arms, sir."

Hardy remarked with a grin, "This Office of Arms is now known as the Office of the Chief Herald of Ireland. It is part of the National Library of Ireland. And I am not a 'Sir.' I never received a knighthood, nor do I ever expect to."

Meghan offered him a thin smile.

Hardy looked at her for the first time with something like warmth. "I rarely take interviews. In addition to my curator's job here, I'm adjunct assistant professor in history at Trinity College, Dublin."

With a nervous smile, she said, "I'm sure you're very busy, and if—"

"No. I'm sorry," Hardy interrupted. "With that *sir* business, I didn't mean to strike a sour note, because… I read your book."

Her eyebrows shot up. *"The House of Sleep?"*

"Indeed, yes. My mother died a few years ago in a nursing home in Laytown, the small community village up along the coast. You were spot on when you reported that nursing home neglect can result in health problems and even death—and that's what happened to her," he said simply. He drew a deep breath and let it out slowly. "So, I'm in your debt. How can I help you?"

"I'm writing a book about the theft of the Irish Crown Jewels, and I wanted to see the actual crime scene and get a floor plan."

She heard hammering in the background.

Hardy said, "The library that housed the Irish Crown Jewels is undergoing refurbishment. The Bedford Tower and the rest of the building will be maintained as much as possible. But, inside the main building, the rooms will be redecorated like any corporate office in Ireland—cubicles, fluorescent lighting, institutional-colored walls. But the outside of the buildings is protected and still intact for the tourists."

Meghan asked, "Can I see the safe in the library?"

"It's not here now. The Ratner safe from which the jewels were stolen is in the Músaem an Gharda Síochána." He smiled. "The Garda Museum is a police museum located in the Treasury Building in the back of the castle."

She shrugged and flipped through her notes. "I've read most of all the information now available. This theft is like an endless shell game."

Hardy said, "There are some theories about why they were stolen. Just theories."

"Please tell me."

"I wouldn't want to try to guess, love. I'm not surprised that His Majesty was embarrassed. On his brief visit to Ireland, he had made his displeasure at their disappearance manifestly clear to Lord Aberdeen. They were, after all, the Crown Jewels, and had been a gift from his granduncle William IV to the Knights of St. Patrick. The King felt their loss and took a keen interest in the investigation into their disappearance."

"So, what in your opinion was the reason for the robbery?"

"One motive might be that the theft was a symbolic political statement by a republican group targeting British authority in Ireland."

She looked puzzled. "Explain?"

"Have you heard of the Irish Republican Brotherhood?"

"No."

"The Bráithreachas Phoblacht na hÉireann was a secret oath-bound fraternal organization dedicated to the establishment of an Independent Democratic Republic in Ireland. That this republican group conspired to steal the King's jewels may seem far-fetched, but you must consider the depth of their animosity to British rule."

"Seriously?"

"It's also possible a clique of unionist officials stole the jewels to embarrass Lord Aberdeen, the King's Viceroy in Ireland. Aberdeen was a known nationalist and advocate for home rule. Unionists feared home rule would result in Catholic dominion over Ireland. As Protestants, the unionists were the minority, happy with the status quo. They didn't want things to change. To deal with Aberdeen, they hatched a plan to steal the jewels just before King Edward VII arrived in Ireland, which they hoped would result in Aberdeen's dismissal. Perhaps they blackmailed Shackleton into obtaining a key, or maybe Vicars provided the key, as he was also a unionist. What happened to the jewels afterwards was unimportant to the unionists. They didn't need the money and couldn't risk being caught selling them. Maybe they placed them in a security box at a bank, where they remain to this day."

He paused. "If you give me a minute, I'll show you the floor plans."

"I would be very grateful."

After a few minutes, Hardy returned. He unfolded a paper drawing and marked the floor plans with a pencil. "This was the first floor of the Office of Arms in our file. I marked in the library with the safe, the strongroom, William Stivey's small office, and the one for Sir Arthur Vicars."

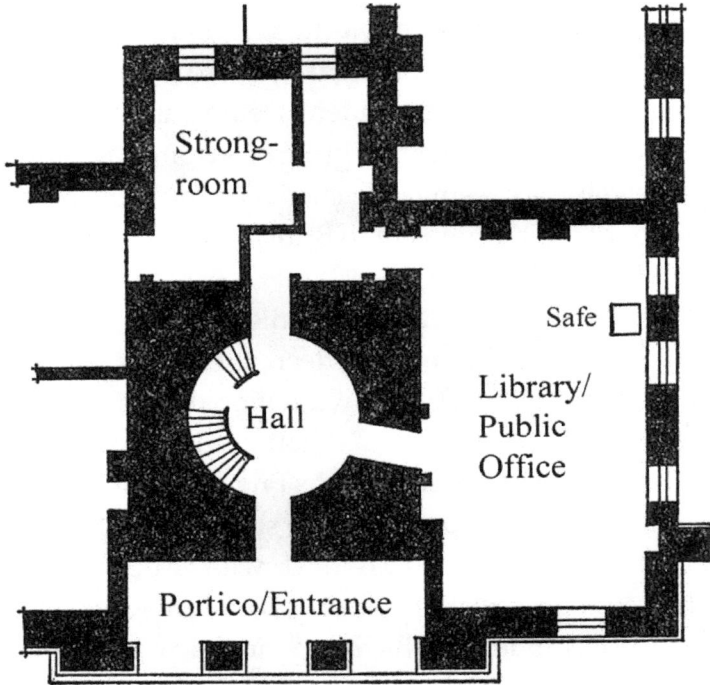

"What happened here?" Meghan asked.

"From what I've been able to understand about the theft, there was no forced entry. Armed guards on duty and police officers inspected the premises every night."

Meghan frowned. "Dr. Hardy, you're the curator of Dublin Castle. How could someone possibly steal the jewels? Why wasn't it ever solved?"

He knowingly said, "The King's intrusion in the affair. That's it."

"That's it? Please tell me."

"King Edward VII was unnerved by the shocking rumors about the friends of his brother-in-law, the Duke of

Argyll. There was a massive scandal in Germany the previous year. A German journalist, a fierce critic of Kaiser Wilhelm II, repeatedly accused members of the Kaiser's cabinet and social circle of homosexual acts. Accusations bounced back and forth, and many in Kaiser Wilhelm's inner circle were forced to resign. Wilhelm was King Edward's nephew, and he absolutely did not want to suffer a similar scandal himself."

Hardy nodded. "And that's why the investigation was *inconclusive*."

Meghan nodded. She supposed that made sense.

He maintained a faint smile. "Did you know Arthur Conan Doyle was connected to the theft of the Irish Crown Jewels? He was a distant cousin of Sir Arthur Vicars, the man responsible for the security of the jewels. Arthur Conan Doyle's involvement was limited to supporting Vicars. Some believe that Doyle's 1908 Sherlock Holmes story 'The Adventure of the Bruce-Partington Plans' was inspired by the theft."

"You're hedging."

"Did you ever read the Arthur Conan Doyle novel *The Sign of the Four*?"

"No."

"In the book, Sherlock Holmes said, 'When you have eliminated the impossible, whatever remains, *however improbable*, must be the truth.' If you want your book to be a winner, you need to investigate the suspects and uncover their motive."

"Easy to say. How would I do that?"

Bryce Hardy smiled. "You need to explore the scandal, conspiracy, and cover-ups, and perhaps then you'll be able to solve the greatest unsolved heist in Irish history." He added, "It's elementary, my dear."

...15

SUSPECTS

THAT EVENING, AFTER MEGHAN arrived home, and after fortifying herself with a strong Merlot wine, she was inclined to agree with Dr. Hardy that this theft must be the most intriguing unsolved robbery in Irish history. With the King and so much else connected with the case, it was cloaked in mystery.

She took out her notebook and listed the suspects, drawn from Owen Kerr's journal, Inspector John Kane's suspicions, and the Vice-Regal Commission's archives.

O'Farrell, Mary
Goldney, Francis
Gorges, Richard
Haddo, Lord George
Kerr, Owen
Mahoney, Pierce Gun
Shackleton, Richard

These people were all related to the Office of Arms in some fashion. No guards would have been suspicious seeing them entering or leaving Dublin Castle. At this juncture, Meghan eliminated O'Keefe, Stivey, and Burtchaell. No one had ever advanced a credible theory to suggest these people were involved.

She looked for the culprit's motive. How would anyone have benefited from the theft? Most Irish newspapers, and even Sir Arthur Vicars, had suggested the prime suspect was Francis Shackleton. He was in financial difficulty and had the opportunity to obtain the key and make a copy. He was, however, out of the country at the time of the theft. Another idea was that Shackleton was the mastermind behind the theft, and his friend, Captain Richard Howard Gorges, a rather unscrupulous character, had carried out the job. However, Meghan rejected the Shackleton-Gorges hypothesis. Having a theory and being able to prove it were two different things.

Meghan knew her book would be prized if it were attentive to detail. She wanted to arrange events in chronological order after 6 July 1907, and then maybe she could solve the greatest unsolved heist in Irish history.

…16

THE TIMELINE

MEGHAN REVIEWED HER INVESTIGATIVE information about the jewel robbery as she drank a cup of black tea and mused how best to describe the theft, the scandal, and the political cover-up. She understood that the theft had never benefitted Vicars; it humiliated him and eventually ruined his career.

She felt Sir Arthur Vicars was caught in the very center of the storm. He had keys to the safe. He could not hold his drink and passed out at parties. He'd authorized his nephew, Pierce Gun Mahoney, to have keys to the Office of Arms and the strongroom. Frank Shackleton shared his residence in St. James's Terrace. Shackleton had invited Richard Gorges as a guest, and Francis Goldney had also stayed in Vicars's home on occasion.

Inspector John Kane had said the theft was an inside job. Vicars's cadre. One or two of them were the offenders responsible for the jewel theft. The sealing order was now removed from under the Official Secrecy Act. She needed to carefully review the report of the Vice-Regal Commission as well as the *Irish Times*, *London Times* and other newspapers reporting on Vicars.

Meghan flipped through her notes, files, internet and press reports on Vicars. She found that Arthur Vicars was born in Leamington Spa, Warwickshire, 27 July 1862, the youngest child of Colonel William Vicars of the 61st Regiment of Foot. Sir Arthur Vicars became a British-Irish genealogist and heraldic expert, known for his role as the

Ulster King of Arms, the principal herald of Ireland. He was knighted by the King in 1896 for his services in heraldry.

In her timeline she listed 6 July 1907: Date of the discovery of the jewel robbery, and the next day a headline in the *Times* read:

The Jewel Robbery at Dublin Castle

The Office of Arms where the jewels were kept is exactly opposite to the state entrance to the Vice-Regal Apartments in the Upper Castle Yard. Just round the corner of the building, a soldier and a policeman are on duty by night and day, and a few yards away at the entrance to the Chief Secretary's Office, another policeman is stationed during office hours. The headquarters of the Dublin Metropolitan Police, the headquarters of the Dublin detective force, the headquarters of the Royal Irish Constabulary, and the head office of the Dublin military garrison are all within a radius of 50 yards of the Office of Arms. In a word, there is no spot in Dublin, or possibly in the United Kingdom, which is at all hours of the 24 more constantly and systematically occupied by soldiers and policemen... Some person got access to the safe... and escaped without leaving any trace behind him.

Meghan was also able to locate a picture from the *Irish Times* of Lord Aberdeen greeting the King, Queen, and Princess Victoria on the 10 July visit to Ireland.

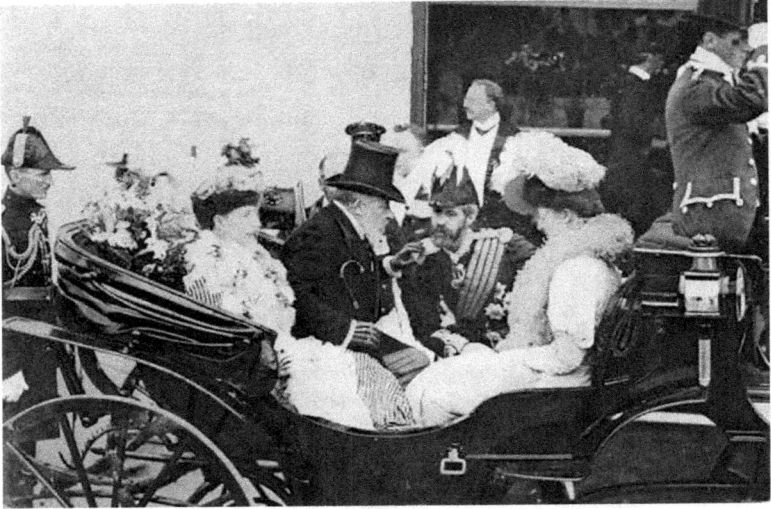

Meghan also found in her files that Superintendent Lowe had sent a report on the robbery to the office of Augustine Birrell, the Chief Secretary of Ireland, on 9 July 1907. From it, she could discern the direction the investigation was taking concerning Sir Arthur Vicars.

Sir Arthur Vicars seems very positive about having locked this safe on the last occasion before the larceny. He appears disposed to think that some expert thief had succeeded in opening it by a false key. This theory is hardly borne out by the circumstances. It appears improbable that any outside person who knew nothing of the building could gain access without leaving marks behind indicating how the entrance had been affected. The facts as presently known would appear to indicate that the larceny was committed by some person familiar with the place who had ordinary means of access and was aware that the jewels were kept there. I should also state that a case containing valuable diamonds, the private property of Sir Arthur Vicars, was also stolen, but no proper description of these articles is yet available.

Inquiries have been made from the constables on duty in the vicinity of the Upper Castle Yard, but nothing of a suspicious nature appears to have come to their knowledge. The matter is being pursued vigorously, and any information obtained will be at once reported.

Superintendent Lowe

On 14 July 1907, another London daily newspaper, the *Gaelic American*, claimed that the government knew the identity of the thief and was simply framing Vicars. They referred to the arrival from London of a Scotland Yard detective. After a few days he unraveled the mystery, and the case was promptly taken out of his hands. The Scotland Yard Inspector had found out too much and was sent home at once. To find out more than was wanted was a very bad thing for a detective to do in a case of this sort. The paper then explained why Shackleton was allowed to get away with the crime. The cover-up was because of Shackleton's connection with the Duke of Argyll, the King's brother-in-law. If Shackleton was arrested, he could tell a story that would make Edward VII blush. On the following day an editorial in the *Daily Express* reported the King's arrival.

The Royal Visit

From press reporting the royal visit seemed to have gone well. However, from exchanges with senior government officials, the theft of the Crown Jewels had enraged the King and embarrassed the Irish administration. For the theft to have occurred in Dublin Castle proved humiliating enough, but when it stole attention from the royal tour, it only further fueled the King's fury. By the third day of his visit, Edward felt that he had endured enough injury, and before leaving Ireland he commanded Lord Aberdeen to fire the people in charge.

Meghan saw a reward in the *Times* on 16 July 1907. She recalled that Owen Kerr had written in his journal, "Sir David Harrel had suggested it to Commissioner Ross."

STOLEN

In August, the newspaper *The Lepracaun* published an illustration entitled "THE GREAT JEWEL ROBBERY." It depicted a stout, well-dressed man, presumably the robber, walking confidently past several figures, including what appeared to be a police officer, amidst an arched doorway of Dublin Castle.

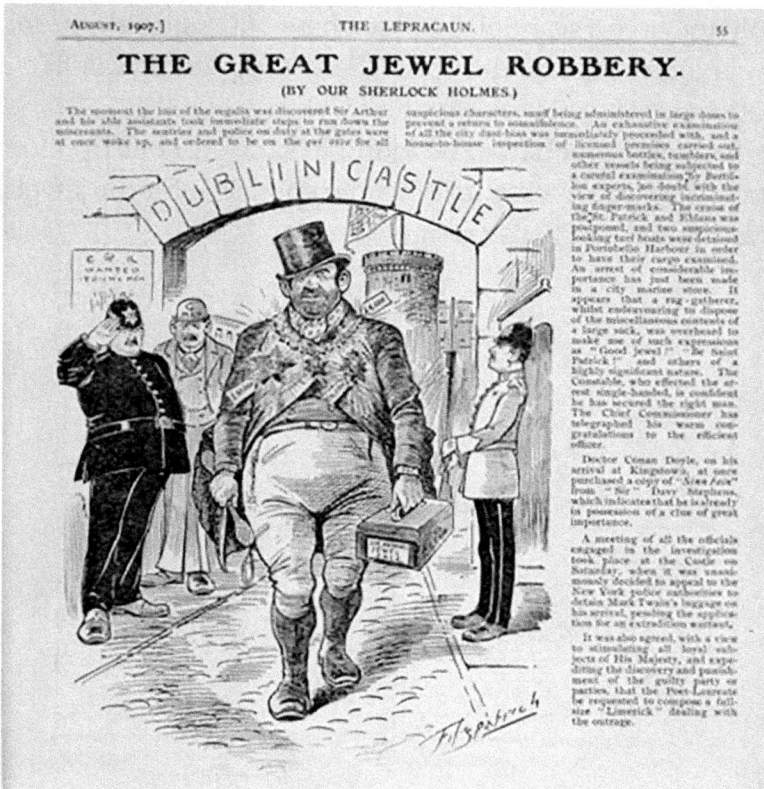

When Meghan visited Dublin Castle, Bryce Hardy had believed King Edward VII, on his brief visit to Ireland, made his displeasure at the jewels' disappearance manifestly clear to Lord Aberdeen. They were, after all, the Crown Jewels, and had been a gift from his granduncle William IV to the Knights of St. Patrick. The King felt their loss and took a keen interest in the investigation into their disappearance.

Meghan read an article by Filson Young, a Northern Irish journalist, published in *The Saturday Review on* 30 September 1907. Young reported from a knowing source in Buckingham Palace: "King Edward held up his hand. 'I will not have a scandal. I will not have mud stirred up, and the matter must be dropped.' And dropped it was like a hot potato."

A scapegoat had to be found to satisfy public opinion, and Sir Arthur Vicars, an official responsible for the jewels, was told he had better resign.

PART IV

THE SCAPEGOAT

...17

ENTER O'MAHONEY

ARISING OUT OF THE DECISION taken by the administration officials and with the King's acquiescence, Meghan read, Sir Arthur Vicars received the following letter on 23 October 1907, signed by the Assistant Under Secretary for Ireland.

Sir,

I am directed by the Lord Lieutenant to inform you that His Excellency has received from the King His Majesty's approval of the reconstitution of the Office of Arms, Dublin Castle. This will involve your being relieved of the office of Ulster which you now hold. I am therefore to request you to make immediate arrangements for relinquishing the duties of your office.

J.B. Dougherty

Meghan assumed his removal from office might have accelerated Sir Arthur Vicars's disgrace. She knew he was alone in his agony. If he accepted his summary dismissal and pension, there would be no inquiry, and Lord Haddo's reputation would remain intact. In those days, events such as these required a sacrificial victim. Vicars was the obvious candidate. The scapegoat.

Aberdeen's letter was the culmination of a process that had begun shortly after the theft. Owen Kerr had written in his journal that Vicars's erratic behavior since 6 July had not impressed the Metropolitan Police. Meghan was surprised, from the news reporting she had read, that the removal letter had had an opposite effect; it galvanized him. The idea that Vicars would fight the King's displeasure had never entered the mind of anyone amongst the bureaucracy of Dublin Castle. As far as Lord Aberdeen and his staff were concerned, Sir Arthur had been dismissed and that was that. An unpleasant episode in the unpleasant history of the castle was closed.

More immediately, Sir Arthur waited on the arrival of his brother, The O'Mahoney of Kerry, to help him fight off his dismissal. The O'Mahoney, rushing home from Bulgaria, telegraphed Sir Arthur to cling to his post until he returned. If he lost office before then, he had little hope of a remedy.

From recorded documents, Perce Charles O'Mahoney arrived in Dublin on 1 November 1907. No sooner had he landed than he went to Sir Arthur's home to hear the latest news. Sir Arthur's account of his curt dismissal drove O'Mahoney into a rage. However, his half-brother conveniently omitted any mention of a sexual scandal.

Unaware of the moral slurs circulating in Dublin, O'Mahoney declared to the press that the authorities had wronged his brother, and family honor demanded that he right this wrong. With his warring spirit fully aroused, The O'Mahoney set out to confront the Irish administration.

Apparently, O'Mahoney's arguments so impressed English Prime Minister Gladstone and his advisors that they felt compelled to hold some sort of inquiry. To compromise with the King, Gladstone requested a Vice-Regal Commission, to which his Majesty consented.

...18

THE VICE-REGAL COMMISSION

MEGHAN FOUND A REPORT published by the HMSO (Her Majesty's Stationery Office) of the Vice Regal Commission appointed to investigate the circumstances and the loss of the Crown Jewels. She took a yellow highlighter pen and marked copies of the documents she was most interested in.

On 10 January 1908, the setting for the confrontation between Vicars and his accusers was suitably modest in the library of the Office of Arms, Dublin Castle. It was not often that a commission sat at the very scene of the crime. The long table in the middle of the library had been removed for the occasion, and a blazing coal fire took the winter chill from the room. The safe had not been moved; it still stood in its corner.

However, the task entrusted to the Vice-Regal Commission appointed by Lord Aberdeen, General Governor of Ireland, was not to conduct a criminal investigation about the jewel theft, but to determine whether Sir Arthur Vicars, the Ulster King of Arms in charge of the Office of Arms in Dublin Castle, had exercised due vigilance and proper care as the custodian of the star and badge.

At eleven o'clock on that Friday morning, the room was crowded. The three commissioners—Shaw, Starkie, and Jones—were seated behind a table. To one side of them was the Solicitor General, Redmond Barry, the man who, ultimately, would be questioning the witnesses. On the other side sat Mr. C.T. Beard, Secretary to the Commission, a shorthand writer recording the inquiry. Outside the Bedford Tower was a group of reporters trying to keep warm while they waited to be allowed in.

Meanwhile, the inquiry started to hear evidence over the six days they were in session, first from Sir George Holmes of the Board of Works about why the safe was not placed in the strongroom; from William Stivey, now ensconced in a Wesleyan Soldiers' Home in Newbridge, County Kildare; from Mrs. Mary O'Farrell; and also from Sir John Ross, Detective Owen Kerr, Sir David Harrel, Pierce Gun Mahoney, Francis Goldney, Francis Shackleton, and Scotland Yard Inspector John Kane.

PUBLISHED REPORT: Examination of Sir John Lowe

Sir John Ross confirmed to the Solicitor-General that he heard about the robbery on Saturday between three and four o'clock, when William Stivey, the office messenger, came for him. He came at once to the library, where he found Sir Arthur Vicars, Mr. Mahoney, and Mr. Burtchaell. He was the first police officer to arrive on the scene.

Solicitor-General: "Superintendent Lowe, when you were summoned to Bedford Tower and as soon as you entered this room, did Sir Arthur Vicars address you?"

Lowe: "He was standing over at the safe here, and he raised his head and said, 'A burglary has been committed here right under our very nose.' I asked him what was robbed, and he said, 'The jewels have been stolen from this safe, also a number of other things, collars. In fact,' he said, 'a clean sweep has been made of the safe.'"

Solicitor-General: "Did he then tell you how the discovery came about?"

Lowe: "Yes. He said that he sent the office messenger, Stivey, with a collar which had been returned, belonging to the late Lord de Ros; he gave it to him in his office upstairs and gave him the key of the safe, or that bunch which had the key of the safe, pointing out the key of the safe to him, and told him to bring it down and put it in the safe; and that Stivey came down and told him he found the safe unlocked and it was empty."

Solicitor-General: "Did you see the case from which the jewels were taken?"

Lowe: "The case was shown to me, all the cases were taken out of the safe and shown to me, including the case in which the jewels were contained."

Solicitor-General: "Can you tell us who has keys to the Office of Arms?

Lowe: "No police officer has a key for any door except Detective Kerr has a key for the outer door because he inspects each night."

PUBLISHED REPORT: Examination of Detective Owen Kerr

Solicitor-General: "Detective Kerr, when on Saturday did you hear something was wrong in the office?"

Kerr: "Well, about ten minutes or fifteen past four."

Solicitor-General: "Who was here?"

Kerr: "Sir Arthur Vicars was here, Sir David Harrel, Superintendent Lowe, Mr. Mahoney, and, I think, Mr. Burchaell and Stivey."

Solicitor-General: "Had the theft of the jewels been reported to you?"

Kerr: "No, sir."

Solicitor-General: "On that occasion, on Saturday when you came into this room, do you remember how Sir Arthur Vicars addressed you?"

Kerr: "I do, sir. He said, 'Kerr, the jewels are all gone; some of the smart boys that have been over for the King's visit made a clean sweep of them.'"

Solicitor-General: "Did he tell you how the safe was unlocked?"

Kerr: "I did not think it proper to ask; my superior officers were present."

Solicitor-General: "Did you know the safe contained the Crown Jewels?"

Kerr: "I had no knowledge that the jewels were there."

Solicitor-General: "Did you make any examination at all on Friday evening to see whether the safe was locked or not?"

Kerr: "I saw the handle in its normal position, always locked."

Solicitor-General: "Did you also see the strongroom door Friday night?"

Kerr: "I did, sir."

Solicitor-General: "Open or locked?"

Kerr: "It was closed and bolted, and I am sure it was locked."

Solicitor-general: "Did you notice anything suspicious?"

Kerr: "No, sir."

*   *   *

ON MONDAY MORNING the commission reconvened. The fire, once again, burned brightly in the grate. They interviewed Mary O'Farrell and William Stivey. Mrs. Farrell was still employed as a cleaner in the Office of Arms; the shake-up had not affected her. She told the commissioners that she discovered the strongroom door open on the morning of Saturday, 6 July. She even talked about the mysterious visitor of March 1907. This is where she held back.

Solicitor General: "Can you identify the visitor?"

O'Farrell: "No, sir."

Meghan felt Mary O'Farrell's response had all the hallmarks of the police coaching her, as mentioned in Kerr's journal. The questioning of William Stivey went on for over an hour. In truth, he did little more than confirm what the commissioners had already known. Then it was Burtchaell's turn.

PUBLISHED REPORT: George Burtchaell

Solicitor-General: Mr. Burtchaell, the present room we are sitting in is the library of the Office of Arms. Am I correct?"

Burtchaell: "Yes."

Solicitor-General: "And you see the safe?"

Burtchaell: "Yes."

Solicitor-General: "The safe in which the Crown Jewels were deposited?"

Burtchaell responded, "Yes," for the third time.

Solicitor-General: "Was there any doorkeeper at all to watch over it?"

Burtchaell grabbed at the proffered straw. "The messenger, Stivey."

Solicitor-General: "But where did Stivey sit?"

Burtchaell: "In his room at the back. The door was opposite, always open, and nobody could come in without his seeing."

Meghan had been in the library and seen the plans. Burtchaell was clearly bluffing. He was doing his best for Vicars. She knew Stivey did not have a clear view of the front door. The solicitor-general said Burtchaell was not telling the truth and dismissed him.

PUBLISHED REPORT: Examination of Francis Goldney

Solicitor-General: "Now, Mr. Goldney, you have told us that you only stayed in Dublin three days at the time you came on the opening of the Exhibition. Did you see the Crown Jewels when you came here?"

Goldney: "Yes."

Solicitor-General: "Did any other people see them on that occasion?"

Goldney: "Yes; Lady Donegall and Lady Orford, and another lady, a friend of Lady Donegall's. Sir Arthur

Vicars asked them if they would like to see the State Rooms and the other things in the castle, and we went over to the State Rooms, and when we came back to the library, Sir Arthur showed us the jewels."

Solicitor-General: "In other words, Sir Arthur Vicars volunteered to show these ladies the jewels?"

Goldney: "Whether these ladies asked to see the jewels or not, I do not know. I know they appeared to be greatly interested in what they saw. I remember Lady Orford saying that she thought it a great pity the jewels should be shut up in a place like this, and I remember Sir Arthur Vicars saying that since his time, the strongroom had been built to keep them protected."

Solicitor-General: "But the safe wasn't in the strongroom. Was this information confidentially disclosed by Sir Arthur to those ladies?"

Goldney: "Well, I would not say it was confidentially disclosed."

Meghan read in the report that Pierce Gun Mahoney seated himself opposite the commissioners to answer Barry's questions, but he was not easily drawn out. His replies were informative and honest, but largely monosyllabic. She felt it was as if he didn't wish to attract too much attention to himself.

Mahoney might have had a valid reason; he was, after all, the only herald who had survived unscathed. Where he could possibly give a straight "yes" or "no" answer, he did just that, only fleshing out his answers when directly requested to do so. He was ill at ease for a man so familiar with the surroundings in which he was giving evidence.

After an hour, Mahoney was allowed to step down. He was followed by John O'Keefe, the Board of Works official responsible for the light in Bedford Tower and who professed not to have known about the crown jewels.

PUBLISHED REPORT: Examination of Sir David Harrel

Solicitor-General: "Assistant Commissioner Harrel, there was an article in the *Irish Times* on 9 July that I will read to you. Is this information correct?

"The headquarters of the Dublin Metropolitan Police, the headquarters of the Royal Irish Constabulary, and the head office of the Dublin military garrison are all within a radius of fifty yards of the safe in the Office of Arms. In a word, there is no spot in Dublin, or possibly in the United Kingdom, which at all hours of the twenty-four, is more constantly occupied by soldiers and policemen."

Harrel: "Yes. That information is true."

Solicitor-General: "As you well know, some person got access to the safe and escaped without leaving any trace. Would you explain to the Commission what system is adopted for guarding the castle and the Offices of Arms, so that robbery could never happen?"

Harrel: "First, at the main gate, there is always a military guard both day and night, and there is always a sentry on duty who walks up and down just outside the Office of Arms. There are three other gates: the Main gate, the Lower Castle Yard gate, and the Ship Street gate. There is the military guard at the main gate, but at each of the other gates, and at the main gate only, there is a policeman on duty throughout the 24 hours every day.

The military are responsible for the closing of the wheeled traffic, which they do at sundown. When that is done, the gates are locked, and a constable has charge of the wicket gates, and as regards the Ship Street gate, it is closed entirely and there is no traffic allowed."

Solicitor-General: "Who has keys to the Office of Arms door?"

Harrel: "I believe there are three or four keys: Mrs. O'Farrell, the cleaning woman; Detective Kerr, who inspects the premises at night; O'Keefe, the Board of Works official; and Sir Arthur Vicars."

Solicitor-General: "Were you aware that Mrs. O'Farrell told us about the mysterious visitor of March 1907?"

Harrel: "Yes, I knew about that."

Solicitor-General: "Who do you think it might have been?"

Harrel: "I don't know."

Meghan knew David Harrel had lied, because it was Lord Haddo that Mary O'Farrell saw in the library. Harrel's negative answer to the Commission tried to protect Lord Aberdeen and King Edward VII from the homosexual revelations in their family.

*   *   *

ON 16 JANUARY 1908, FRANCIS SHACKLETON gave evidence to the commission.

PUBLISHED REPORT: Examination of Francis Shackleton

Solicitor-General: "Can you tell us, Mr. Shackleton, at what date you took up your residence in St. James's Terrace with Sir Arthur Vicars?"

Shackleton: "The move was made in September or the end of August 1905. I remember that I spent about two months in Dublin during the two years all put together."

Solicitor-General: "Mr. Shackleton, Sir Arthur Vicars claims the suspicion for the theft has been thrown on you. I must ask you a definite question, and you will understand that you need not answer it if you do not like. Did you, or did you not, take the jewels?"

Shackleton: "I did not take them. I know nothing of their disappearance."

Solicitor-General: "Were you directly or indirectly involved in their taking?"

Shackleton: "I had no hand in it, nor do I know anybody that took them."

Solicitor-General: "Can you assist our Commission in any way?"

Shackleton: "Not in any way, sir. I have absolutely no knowledge of it. I cannot even suggest a possible solution of it, other than the one which I have already suggested, namely, that some resident in our house at some period had access to the key."

Solicitor-General: "Have you heard as to who that might be?"

Shackleton: "No, sir; other than Lord Haddo had taken them on a previous occasion."

*   *   *

MEGHAN READ THAT SHACKLETON had more of Vicars's charges thrown at him.

Solicitor-General: "Sir Arthur's belief is that you returned to Dublin from 28 to 30 June, stayed in a Dublin hotel, and took your Office of Arms front-door key and stole the jewels."

Shackleton: "The police accounted for most of my movements in the few days preceding the theft."

As the interrogation continued, Meghan read that Francis Shackleton began to drop important names. He made no secret of his friendship with the King's brother-in-law, the Duke of Argyll. He adopted a posture of disarming frankness when he was asked about his access to Vicars's keys.

Shackleton: "I could easily have taken possession of the safe key while Vicars was taking a bath or was otherwise occupied."

Meghan knew these admissions helped his credibility and did nothing at all to assist Vicars's case. The solicitor general suggested as much, and Shackleton was excused. Then Scotland Yard Chief Inspector John Kane testified at the inquiry.

Solicitor-General: "Did you ever trace any fact that would tend to throw suspicion on Mr. Shackleton?"

John Kane: "Never."

Solicitor-General: "Not a shred of evidence against him?"

John Kane: "Not the remotest. I dismissed Vicars's allegations outright. Shackleton had a perfect alibi for the time—he could not have taken the jewels."

*   *   *

THE COMMISSION'S REPORT was given to Lord Aberdeen on 16 January 1908, and it was published in the newspapers 31 January.

Your Majesty:
Although it was no part of our duty under Your Excellency's Warrant to conduct a criminal investigation into the robbery of the jewels, or to take evidence with a view to the ascertainment of the thief, yet as, on the evidence given before us and now in print, it appears that the name of Mr. Francis Richard Shackleton was more than once named as that of the probable or possible author of this great crime, we think it only due to that gentleman to say that he came from San Remo at great inconvenience to give evidence before us, that he appeared to us to be a perfectly truthful and candid witness, and that there was no evidence whatever before us which would support the suggestion that he was the person who stole the jewels.
Having fully investigated all the circumstances connected with the loss of the Regalia of the Order of St. Patrick, and having examined and considered carefully the

arrangements of the Office of Arms in which the Regalia were deposited, and the provisions made by Sir Arthur Vicars, or under his direction, for their safekeeping, and having regard especially to the inactivity of Sir Arthur Vicars on the occasions immediately preceding the disappearance of the jewels, when he knew that the office and the strongroom had been opened at night by unauthorized persons, we feel bound to report to Your Excellency that, in our opinion, Sir Arthur Vicars did not exercise due vigilance or proper care as the custodian of the Regalia.

We desire to express our obligations to our Secretary, Mr. C.T. Beard, of the Chief Secretary's office, for the valuable assistance he gave us in the conducting of our inquiry. All which we humbly submit for Your Excellency's consideration.

—James J. Shaw, Robert F. Starkie, Chester Jones

The same day as the commission's report was appearing in the newspapers, Meghan read that the *Irish Times* carried a letter from Vicars in which he outlined the history of the attempts to dismiss him. The *Irish Times*, no lover of the Liberal administration in Ireland, offered some editorial sympathy. The paper claimed to hold no brief for Vicars but criticized the gossip and scandalous stories that were doing the rounds as well as the accusations against the Irish government that "it was more anxious to hush up the loss of the jewels than to secure their recovery."

Meghan concluded that, despite extensive investigations, including involvement from Scotland Yard, the commission was unable to definitively identify who had stolen the jewels. She believed the Vice-Regal

Commission was a star chamber, carefully arranged to ignore the theft and the homosexuality scandal, but to placate King Edward VII, and to have a political scapegoat for the theft—Sir Arthur Vicars.

"I don't want to hush the bloody affair," she mumbled. "I want to expose the people who took the jewels, and Chief Inspector Kane concluded that the crime was committed with the aid of an insider, which can only imply the thief was a part of Sir Arthur Vicars's cadre."

She listed the suspects: Mary O'Farrell, Francis Goldney, Richard Gorges, Lord George Haddo, Detective Owen Kerr, Pierce Gun Mahoney, Richard Shackleton.

"Bugger it all," Meghan said. "Now which one did it?"

PART V

FINGERS OF SUSPICION

...19

MARY O'FARRELL

FROM HER BACKGROUND INFORMATION, Meghan started with the cleaning woman. Mary O'Farrell would have been in her forties when the theft happened. In the late 1890s, her husband was working for Guinness and had a problem with alcohol. He moved to America and died of alcoholism, leaving her with four sons. One subsequently died in an accident. To make a living she had been forced to allow the other three to be housed in an orphanage.

In 1907, Mary O'Farrell got a job as a cleaning woman in the Office of Arms. Then she was reunited with her children in a modest flat in the Iveagh Buildings around the corner from Dublin Castle. Each of her boys was expected to help put in some domestic chores associated with the Office of Arms.

She'd told Detective Owen Kerr that Wednesday, 3 July, should not have been an exceptional day. She arrived at the Office of Arms shortly before eight o'clock, as she did every day during the summer. Having passed the patrolling sentries, she reached the Bedford Tower and took out her latchkey to open the front door. As Mrs. O'Farrell pushed her key into the latch, the door swung open. Surprised, she entered the building warily. The catch could have been left on from the previous night by accident, or one of the office staff might have decided to start work bright and early—though neither had ever happened before. A cautious search revealed that the building was empty. She waited until Stivey, the messenger, came in and told him what had happened.

On Saturday, 6 July, a still more startling incident occurred. Mrs. O'Farrell said she opened the office at her usual hour and walked into the messenger's room to see if any written message had been left for her. On entering the messenger's room, she found the outer door of the strongroom was standing ajar. There were two keys hanging in the lock of the grille. She took these two keys out of the grille lock, shut the outer door of the strongroom, and put the keys on the messenger's desk. She told Detective Kerr that with a stub of pencil she always carried with her, she wrote a message on Stivey's blotting pad.

"Mr. Stivey, I found the strongroom door open this morning. I closed the gate and am leaving the keys on your table." She waited nearly half an hour for the messenger to arrive, but then had to leave to do her weekend shopping. That's when the theft was discovered.

*   *   *

MEGHAN WAS ABLE TO LOCATE an undated, annotated typescript draft of Robert Brennan's novel *The Theft of the Crown Jewels: A Dublin Castle Mystery*, bound in its original folder. Brennan had researched the theft in earnest. Part of his information came from Seamus, the eldest son of Mrs. Mary O'Farrell. Seamus O'Farrell, like Robert Brennan, had taken part in the 1916 Easter Rising. Seamus also became a member of the first Irish Senate and moved in the same political circles as Brennan.

Seamus O'Farrell had told Brennan what he knew. "On Sunday, 7 July, the day after the discovery of the theft, without a warrant, Detective Sergeant Owen Kerr questioned his mother, and she told him about seeing Lord Haddo in the office after Christmas. Then a few days later, Sergeant Kerr again interviewed his mother and browbeat her into retracting her story about seeing Lord Haddo."

Robert Brennan first started writing his non-fiction book, then evidently turned it into a novel, because he had run afoul of the mysterious silence that blanketed the case on both sides of the Irish Sea. Brennan was frustrated and wrote in the *Irish Times*, "Even now after more than 50 years, the mere mention of the case retains the power of afflicting reputedly intelligent persons with a kind of mass amnesia."

In her notes, Meghan wrote, "Detective Sergeant Kerr ruled out Mrs. Mary O'Farrell and William Stivey, because neither of them had access to the keys, except for Stivey, on Saturday, when Sir Arthur Vicars asked him to put a collar in the safe and he discovered the theft."

Meghan listed a motive that Mrs. O'Farrell needed money for her family, but low probability that she was ever involved in the theft. She gave her a pass.

...20

ATHLONE PURSUIVANT

FROM FRANCIS GOLDNEY'S testimony before the Vice-Regal Commission: Major Francis Bennett-Goldney was an antiquary, Member of Parliament (MP) for Canterbury, and former mayor of Canterbury. Goldney was an ambitious man, used to getting what he wanted.

He met Sir Arthur Vicars in 1905 at a meeting of antiquarians. He outright asked Vicars for a position within the office of the Ulster King of Arms. Vicars, a little put out by the aggressiveness, asked for a proper recommendation, which Goldney, thanks to his aristocratic connections, accomplished easily. The Duke of Bedford supplied the recommendation, but it took a while for Goldney to achieve his position.

Goldney was appointed as Athlone Pursuivant of the Order of St. Patrick in February 1907. His duties included assisting in the recording of coats of arms, verifying genealogical records, and participating in state ceremonies.

In Sergeant Owen Kerr's journal, both he and Chief Inspector Kane were suspicious about Goldney's role in the disappearance of the jewels.

*   *   *

WHEN WAR BROKE OUT IN 1914, Goldney was commissioned as a captain in the Army Service Corps. He died on 26 July 1918 in Rouen, France, as a result of injuries sustained in a car accident. He was buried in the St. Sever Cemetery in Rouen.

Meghan found Goldney's portrait published in the *Illustrated London News* on 24 August 1918.

Goldney left no wife or children, and some of his effects were auctioned off after his death. It emerged, however, that some items in his possession did not actually belong to him. In 1921 Canterbury's mayor and corporation made a successful claim for the return of valuable books and documents which Goldney had taken from the city's museum and library. The corporation's counsel hinted at other misdeeds and suggested that Goldney was "a person who was unable to distinguish between his own property and the property of other persons." However, the judge absolved him of any "improper conduct," depicting him as having been careless about returning items he had removed in his capacity as honorary director, rather than being a willful criminal.

Meghan felt Goldney had not been in Ireland between the last date the jewels were seen in June and the discovery of their loss in July, and there was no firm evidence to suggest that he had played any part in the theft of the jewels.

...21

THE CAPTAIN

"RICHARD HOWARD GORGES was born in Boyle, Ireland, in 1874, the son of a prominent Anglo-Irish family. Like his father, he went into the Army."

Meghan Walsh found this information on Wikipedia. She read that Gorges fought in the Second Matabele War in 1896 and joined the Cape Police force in 1897. On his application form for the Cape Police, he falsely claimed he had spent eighteen months in the Royal Canadian Dragoon.

Gorges also fought in the Boer War, first as a trooper with Thorneycroft's Mounted Infantry in November 1899, but he was dishonorably discharged for alleged sodomy. His final posting in South Africa was a lieutenant in the Border Scouts. In November 1902 Richard Gorges was back in Britain, where he joined the 3rd Battalion, Royal Irish Regiment, as an instructor in musketry with the rank of captain.

From Owen Kerr's journal, Meghan recalled him writing, "Sir Arthur Vicars told Inspector Kane he didn't tolerate the erratic Captain Gorges's visits to his home. Vicars considered him a 'morally bad lot.'"

During the war years, Richard Gorges traveled to London and, in the confusion of the urgent recruiting campaign that was in progress, was accepted without question. On 5 September 1914, he was commissioned as a captain in the London Rifle Regiment and was back in uniform again. But by now this hard-drinking professional soldier was a chronic alcoholic. At first, he succeeded in disguising his dunking habits by his vast military experience, but soon it became clear he was of little use to the Army.

After only four months, he was allowed to resign his commission. For the third time in his life, Richard Gorges had been rejected as unfit to serve. He rented rooms in a house in Hampstead, London, telling his landlord that he'd been invalided out of the Army after being gassed in the trenches in Belgium.

According to transcripts from his trial from the Crown Prosecutor: "The defendant claimed, 'On some nights, whatever alcoholic mist I was in, my black depression infuriated me. I would pick up one of my two service revolvers and loose off a volley of shots out my bedroom window into the darkness. It made me feel better.'

"That was what alerted the police," the prosecutor said. "They began to get complaints about Gorges's nocturnal firing of weapons. On 14 July 1915, Detective Sergeant Askew and Detective Constable Arthur Young went to serve a warrant on Gorges in his Hampstead flat; the police officers were unarmed.

"When they confronted Gorges, they asked if they could talk to him privately, but he pulled a second revolver and fired almost point blank at Detective Young. Askew managed to wrestle Gorges to the floor, and with help subdued him. A doctor later pronounced Detective Young dead at the scene."

Meghan read that he was a pathetic sight at his trial. The inquest into Young's death took place on 27 July. An attempt was made to introduce Gorges's medical history in evidence, but the prosecutor was firm in his instructions to the jury: "It was not within the competence of a jury to consider questions of sanity. He was convicted."

Gorges was publicly named by an Irish Member of Parliament, Laurence Ginnell, in a speech he made in the House of Commons on 20 December 1912, under the protection of Parliamentary Privilege. He said, "Richard Gorges, while in South Africa, was a reckless bully, a robber, a murderer, a bugger, and a sod." He also intimated, "Gorges is not being prosecuted for the Dublin Castle jewel robbery in order to conceal crimes—much worse than theft."

"If Gorges had partnered with Frank Shackleton," Meghan thought aloud, "he could very well have been involved in the theft."

...22

THE DETECTIVE SERGEANT

OWEN KERR WAS LISTED AS a possible suspect. The Vice-Regal Commission reported on their suspicions of Detective Kerr after examinations of him on 14 January 1908.

> Detective Owen Kerr confirmed he had been doing duty in connection with Dublin Castle for the past five years. We strongly suspect Kerr but readily concede that evidence is thin. However, if our theory is correct, then the conspirators would have made sure to include their man on the investigating team. Our theory also demanded a man who could go into the Office of Arms with total impunity, and Kerr fits that description perfectly.

Meghan found the journal of Sergeant Kerr extremely important in her search for the truth. He accurately reported, almost daily, the investigation procedure from the day of the theft, which included accounts of Scotland Yard Inspector Kane interviewing the suspects. She disregarded the Vice-Regal Commission reports.

*　　*　　*

REGARDING OWEN KERR, Meghan was unable to find any reference to him after 1907 on the *British News Archives*, the *Irish Times* digital records, or Wikipedia. Her presumption was that Owen Kerr was not alive after 1918.

STOLEN

He may have died in World War I, along with 880,000 other British soldiers. Sadly, she thought that Detective Sergeant Owen Kerr might be buried in an unmarked grave somewhere in France or Belgium.

THE CORK HERALD

FROM PUBLISHED REPORTS, PIERCE GUN MAHONEY was appointed Cork Herald of Arms of the Order of St. Patrick in September 1905. Mahoney lived in Dublin and, as a volunteer, attended the Office of Arms as often as he could. His uncle was Sir Arthur Vicars.

Mahoney affirmed that he was given a latchkey for the outer door of the office and a strongroom key when his uncle was away but had not returned them when Sir Arthur came back from vacation in December 1906.

While Mahoney was friends with Shackleton, Goldney, and Gorges and they had been invited to his uncle Arthur's house many times, he could not have been involved with the theft of the jewels. Pierce Gun Mahoney left Dublin in April for health reasons and didn't return until 4 July. In Owen Kerr's journals, it was noted that John Kane discounted Pierce Gun Mahoney as a suspect.

Later on, after Sir Arthur Vicars had resigned his post after the inquiry, Pierce Gun Mahoney emerged unscathed from the turmoil of the theft. Goldney and Shackleton had resigned earlier, yet Pierce Gun Mahoney, the Cork Herald, surprisingly remained at the Office of Arms for the next three years. Why the Irish administration allowed him stay on after the inquiry is puzzling. More probably, everybody, including the King, had had enough of this dreadful affair.

When the Liberals were re-elected in 1910, Mahoney resigned as Cork Herald. At around that time, he moved from his home in Burlington Road in Dublin to a house belonging to his father in Castleisland, County Kerry. Mahoney belonged to a very old and wealthy Irish clan, which allowed him to live a life of leisure, but not for long.

Meghan read an article in the *Irish Times*, 28 July 1914.

Death of Pierce Gun Mahoney

Pierce Gun Mahoney was visiting his father at Grange Con, County Wicklow, and on Saturday, 26 July, Charles McKutey, the estate manager, saw Mahoney put on a coat and depart in the direction of the lake bordering his father's estate. Mahoney had loaded his shotgun and said he planned to shoot pigeons and rabbits and would be back well before dark. He wasn't missed until much later that evening. After searching, they discovered Mahoney's body partly submerged in the lake about three yards from the bank, his shotgun resting on a low barbed-wire fence that skirted the lake.

The coroner called an inquest into Mahoney's death. The autopsy revealed that the shotgun wounds were not self-inflicted. Strangely, the coroner did not call a police officer to explain the results. The jury at the inquest returned a verdict of accidental death, with no blame being attached to any person. This was charitable, but on the face of it, improbable. Since Mahoney was an experienced hunter, he would hardly have lifted the loaded gun with its two barrels aimed straight at his chest. The motive for foul play remained obscure, and he could just as easily have been shot by a person unknown.

Meghan understood that Pierce Gun Mahoney's acquaintances were suspected of the Crown Jewels robbery and wondered if he had been — silenced.

...24

THE *DUBLIN HERALD*

FROM THE *DICTIONARY OF IRISH BIOGRAPHY*, Meghan unraveled Francis Shackleton's early life in the Army and then after the war, when Sir Arthur Vicars appointed him Dublin Herald.

Shackleton, Francis Richard ("Frank") (1876–1941), Dublin Herald of Arms (1905–7), was born 19 September 1876 in Kilkea, County Kildare. In 1900, Shackleton volunteered for service in the second Boer war and was commissioned as a second lieutenant in the Royal Irish Fusiliers, being promoted to full lieutenant in October 1900. Even though his regiment did not see any action, he was sent out alone on special assignment and was injured and was invalided home. He received the Queen's Medal, recuperated from his injuries in Devon, and then rejoined his regiment.

After the Boer War, he continued his Army career for a brief period. Of a dapper and flamboyant nature, Shackleton moved in society circles and was acquainted with the duke of Argyll and Lord Ronald Sutherland-Gower. He was also a friend of Sir Arthur Vicars, Ulster King of Arms. In 1907 the two men shared a house at 7 St. James's Terrace, Clonskeagh.

Vicars, who ran the Office of Arms as though it was his own private kingdom, secured an appointment for Frank Shackleton as Dublin Herald in September 1905. While serving in this capacity, Shackleton was suspected of involvement in the theft of the Regalia of the Grand Master of the Order of St. Patrick, commonly known as the Irish Crown Jewels.

MEGHAN FOUND ANOTHER POST about Shackleton in the *Irish Times*, 25 October 1913.

Francis Shackleton Arrested

For Francis Shackleton, the Mexican Land and Timber Company was to be his meal ticket for life; if the investment paid off, he stood to make over £70,000. The scheme was a simple one involving the purchase of a vast tract of land in Mexico that would then be exploited for the huge quantities of timber it would provide. If the capital could be found to fund the investment, there was a small fortune to be made.

Shackleton's other business enterprises were sidelines compared to the scale of the Land and Timber Company, but, in addition to his own affairs, Shackleton was also in demand as a sort of informal business manager for some of his friends.

His good fortune couldn't last indefinitely, and his first bad break was the worst. The Mexican scheme at the center of his complex dealings collapsed. The brokers wrote to Shackleton stating that owing to a variety of circumstances, of which the death of King Edward in 1910 was by no means the least, they had decided not to underwrite the Mexican company's shares.

Surprisingly, it wasn't until September 1912 that a warrant was issued for Shackleton's arrest. As is often the case, the indictment related to one of his lesser crimes. He was charged with having fraudulently converted Miss

Browne's £1,000 inheritance cheque. But he avoided prison.

Shackleton had left the jurisdiction, having accepted a job as far away from England as he could get. He was employed in Portuguese West Africa as a plantation manager. It was a hot, oppressive climate, and the work was hard. But it had the advantage of being far out of reach of his English creditors. Or so he thought. When his whereabouts became known, he was arrested by the Portuguese police at Hanha in October 1912. Scotland Yard was informed of his arrest and immediately sent an officer to repatriate him.

On 10 January 1913, Shackleton appeared before Mr. Curtis Bennett at Bow Street Police Court and was formally charged before being remanded on bail of £2,000. As the case progressed, more charges were added. Shackleton was also accused of defrauding Lord Gower of £5,000. Then on 24 October 1913, a verdict of guilty was brought in by the jury after only ten minutes of deliberation. Shackleton was sentenced to jail for fifteen months with hard labor.

After his release from prison, Shackleton's star continued to wane. He changed his name to Mellor and opened an antique shop in Chichester. Residents recalled him being slightly built, with grey hair and a moustache, always neatly suited and hatted, and living in more modest circumstances than he wished.

...25

LORD ABERDEEN'S SON

LORD GEORGE HADDO WAS NOT without suspicion in the theft. Meghan researched and found an article in *The New York Times* of 19 January 1908. The article stated:

> A certain Lord, who is the son of an Earl, is the person whom all Dublin believes could tell how the Crown Jewels were taken from the safe and where they are now. This Lord has a strong animosity toward Sir Arthur Vicars and would be glad to have him turned out of his office. It is said that politics figures distinctly in the regalia affair in which the names of persons of high titles are mentioned. All names may be made public, but a strenuous effort is going on to hush the affair, and it may prove successful.

The New York Times was not the only American paper interested in the Crown Jewels affair. *The Nationalist Newspaper* reported under a bold heading:

Argyll, the King's Brother-in-law

> The Chief Secretary, Mr. Birrell, has described Shackleton as an "abandoned ruffian," yet this abandoned ruffian has been the guest of Lord Haddo at Lord Aberdeen's house and on one occasion left there with the Duke of Argyll, a brother-in-law of His Most Gracious Majesty, Edward VII. If Shackleton and Gorges were arrested, they could tell a story about their titled associates that would make the King blush.

Meghan recalled from Owen Kerr's journal that Chief Inspector Kane had had a hunch and discreetly inquired into Lord Haddo. He learned that Lord Haddo had stayed in Scotland on 6 July, the date the robbery was discovered.

*   *   *

ALTHOUGH THE PRINCIPLE OF GUILT by association is a dangerous one, it had great merit for Meghan's investigation of the theft. She had an instinctive feeling about who had stolen the jewels. A hunch. It was Lord Haddo. As a crime reporter, it was a logical assessment of all the information she had read.

The truth behind the apparent immunity of Shackleton and Gorges from prosecution could well be more mundane. The police may simply have not had enough evidence against them. Kane was very specific about this in a statement before the Vice-Regal Commission. No tangible evidence was found to incriminate Shackleton.

When names such as Lord Gower and the Duke of Argyll were mentioned in relation to Shackleton, the police began to back off and passed the case back to their political superiors. One of the extraordinary features of this case was the silence of the principal characters: Commissioner Ross, Superintendent Lowe, and Chief Secretary Birrell. Lord Aberdeen had left no papers that threw any light on the affair. After King Edward's death, his principal aide, on his master's instruction, had destroyed all the King's sensitive papers.

Meghan believed Sir Arthur Vicars was being victimized to protect Aberdeen's son and King Edward. Finally, she needed to come to terms with Kane's reaction to Shackleton. The Chief Inspector had concluded that the crime had been committed with the aid of an insider, which could only mean one of the heralds or Haddo.

At the time the only herald who had earned a "shady reputation" was Shackleton. How many experienced policemen would have ignored Shackleton and the rumors that he was in financial difficulties as they investigated the theft?

To compound matters, John Kane knew about the homosexual activities of Shackleton and his friends. Kane appeared to have been unusually broad-minded in not allowing any personal prejudice against Shackleton's way of life to interfere with his judgment in the case. Inspector Kane was a thoroughly competent officer.

Although the Kane report had never been made public, she could glean important inferences from his testimony at the Vice-Regal Commission. Kane implied the thief had "forged" the keys and stolen the jewels well before 5 July, and the motive was to create an embarrassment prior to the King's visit. By mentioning a forged key, Kane implied that Sir Arthur was not the thief.

He also vouched for the innocence of Shackleton. Meghan knew that the Irish administration was most distressed over the suspect named in Kane's report and dismissed the Chief Inspector. Thus, the person he named in his report must have had considerable stature in Ireland. Only one remaining person associated with Sir Arthur had the stature and prestige to compel the Irish administration and the Lord Lieutenant to go to such extreme lengths to shield him—that person was Lord Haddo.

Lord Haddo later became an Elder of the Church of Scotland, and when the Liberals prepared to nominate hundreds of peers in the constitutional battles of 1910, Haddo's name was among them. He succeeded to the title and in his later years devoted his life to a multitude of local issues, outlived his two wives, and died in 1965, a much-respected Scottish nobleman.

Now she had a serious problem. If she identified Lord Haddo in her new book, she had no proof, just one-hundred-year-old circumstantial evidence.

She was fucked.

PART VI

THE CLEANING WOMAN'S SECRET

...26

THE DIRECTOR

ON MONDAY MEGHAN'S PHONE BUZZED. Mrs. Maguire, secretary to the *Irish Times* managing director, was on the phone. "Mr. McFarlane would like to see you in his office at ten this morning."

"Of course. I'll be there. What is it about?"

Mrs. Maguire had hung up.

"Feck's sake," Meghan wondered. "What did I do now?"

She rode the Dublin bus to the *Times* office on Tara Street. At ten a.m. she was in Brendan McFarlane's office. He had a jovial face that seemed a mismatch with his dark, penetrating eyes. Seeing Meghan, he beamed with obvious pleasure.

"How's your new book coming along?"

"Not brilliantly. After one hundred years, I believe it's an empty exercise to unearth the person who stole the Crown Jewels."

McFarlane smiled. "So did Scotland Yard, and they had the best chief inspector on the case." He added, "Irish politics are tribal, incestuous, tangled, and perplexing. Maybe this was a political grenade for the King that nobody felt like touching."

Brendan McFarlane pushed his spectacles back up on the bridge of his nose. "I owe you one, lass. When we were prosecuted for offending the Official Secrets Act, you were imprisoned for six months, and I was fined a measly sum."

Meghan nodded.

McFarlane asked, "Do you read the *Sunday Independent* paper?"

"No. I don't."

"Well, Meghan, you might have missed the evidence you were looking for. The *Sunday Independent* reported a filmmaker named Oisín Mistéil's great-great-grandmother was the cleaner who discovered the Irish Crown Jewels theft. Mistéil said his granny held many secrets, and he's filmed her. The documentary will be broadcast next week on TG4, the public service broadcaster. It's called *Ar Thóir na Crown Jewels*."

"That sounds like bullshit."

McFarlane tapped his nose. "I've been a newspaper man for over fifty years, and I think there's something here." He handed her a slip of paper. "Many families have interesting stories tucked away in their history. But this one, you best be interested in. Interview the grandmother; the sooner the better.

"The lady's name is Emer Cosgrove, 98 years old. Her address is written here. She's in Dublin. I checked, and Mrs. Cosgrove is truly the granddaughter of Mary O'Farrell, the cleaner employed by Arthur Vicars."

They stared at each other. "Why?" Meghan asked.

"Don't be daft. Mrs. Cosgrove's father was Seamus O'Farrell, Mary O'Farrell's son. Seamus was part of the Irish Republican Brotherhood."

Meghan closed her eyes and exhaled. "Thank you, Jesus," she whispered.

...27

GRANNY

THE HEAT HAD THICKENED. The early-afternoon sun gripped Dublin. The streets were quiet. When Meghan knocked at Mrs. Cosgrove's door, there was no movement inside, but after a moment, a heavy, slow voice called, "Well, in you come."

Mrs. Cosgrove had deep lines on her forehead. Her gray hair was pulled back in an impossible knot. Her black eyes were sharp and watchful. The front room was cluttered with timeworn furniture, ruffled porcelain objects, and framed photos of popes and family members.

"Hi," Meghan began. "Are you Emer Cosgrove?"

"That's God own truth," she said.

"I'm a writer and a reporter from the *Times*. I heard your grandmother was Mary O'Farrell and your dad Seamus?"

Mrs. Cosgrove snorted, conceding the kinship. "Sit down there now. You'll have a cup of tea and scones, yeah?"

"Yes. Thank you, ma'am."

Mrs. Emer Cosgrove took a few scones out of her freezer, defrosted them in the microwave, and buttered them. Meghan sat on the edge of the slippery sofa. She knew she had to eat the damn scones. She sighed and settled back on the sofa, watching the old lady pour her cup of tea. Mrs. Cosgrove's hands, marked with the soft tremors of age, steadied the teapot with both hands to ensure control.

"Mrs. Cosgrove, the last *Sunday Independent* paper said you were going to be on TV."

She winked at Meghan and laughed, a rusty cackle, but it lit up her face. "That's true. At my age, I'm thrilled to be a part of the documentary."

"Can you tell me why?"

"My grandson works for a film company. Oisín told me the producer was considering doing a program on the disappearance of the Crown Jewels in 1907. Oisín told his boss his granny, me, was the granddaughter of Mary O'Farrell, the cleaner at Dublin Castle at that time, and I ought to be included in the documentary."

"May I ask, what do you remember about your granny?"

Mrs. Emer Cosgrove leaned back in her armchair and laughed. "I was only nine years old." With a faint smile, she related, "My father told me his mother would have been in her 40s when this robbery happened. She was a cook initially.

"Da said in the late 1890s his father, my granda, was working for Guinness. He was a cooper but had a problem with alcohol. He moved to America and died of alcoholism." The old woman gave a shouldered shrug. "So, Granny was left with my father, Seamus, and my uncles. She couldn't work as a cook during the day for watching over her kids. She got a job from Sir Arthur Vicars, which meant she could work in the morning cleaning the Office of Arms. She hated the man. Vicars showed her no respect, acting as if she was worthless or disposable, like literal garbage."

"I'm sorry for that," Meghan said. "Vicars came to a sad end. He was shot."

"For God's sake, don't be telling me that."

There was a long pause.

Meghan said, "Your grandmother discovered the missing Crown Jewels and alerted Vicars. Did you know that?"

"O, begod, of course I do." Mrs. Cosgrove clasped her cardigan together. "'Tis all I've heard from years on."

Meghan took out her notepad and asked, "What did you hear?"

"My father said that Granny was on her morning cleaning rounds in the Office of Arms, and she found that the outer door to the strongroom was unlocked. The key was still sitting in the lock, on a ring with other keys. So, she wrote a note for the messenger, Mr. Stivey, and left the keys on his desk for him. After the theft she heard that Mr. Stivey had tried to put a gold collar in the safe in the library for Vicars, but the safe was unlocked. He hurried back to tell Vicars; then they found the gold collars and the Irish Crown Jewels were completely gone."

Mrs. Cosgrove looked amused. "That's what I heard. Now you have it. What are you going to do with it?"

"I'm writing a book about the missing Crown Jewels and the robbery." Meghan asked, "Are these pictures of your family?"

Emer Cosgrove nodded.

"Your granny doesn't look like a cleaning lady. May I take a picture?"

Then she spotted another photograph. "Is your father in this picture?"

"Da is the second one on the right."

"A handsome fellow. Do you know any of the other men?"

"I'm told the second one on the left was Mr. Girrard, a jeweler in Dublin. As far as I know, his establishment is still here in town."

"Any others?"

She peered through her glasses. "The one on the middle, I think, is Mr. James Connally."

"Who was he?"

Mrs. Cosgrove's eyes darted away. "Don't know."

Meghan reached out and turned the picture over. All that was written was "Bráithreachas Pdoblacht na hÉireann." She noted the jeweler's name and the inscription from the picture, trying to remember the name, but couldn't place it.

"You have been most helpful and a dear," Meghan said. "When my book comes out, you will be the very first to have it."

"More luck to you," Mrs. Cosgrove said. "I'm 98 years old. You better hurry up."

*   *   *

THE GIRRARD AND CO. JEWELRY STORE was housed in a Victorian-style building on Grafton Street. The display windows featured a collection of rings, necklaces, bracelets, and watches. When Meghan entered, she saw a stocky, bespeckled man who asked, "Good afternoon, madam. May I help you?"

"Need a word, if you don't mind. I'm authoring a book about the theft of the Crown Jewels from Dublin Castle. Are you Mr. Girrard?"

She saw a tiny, cynical flick of his eyebrows. "Yes."

"I met with Mrs. Cosgrove, Mary O'Farrell's granddaughter. She had pictures of her family. I took one on my iPhone. She told me her father, Seamus, was on the second right, and she believed this one on the second left was your grandfather."

Girrard's eyes darted to the picture on her phone. "Why, yes. I think that's so."

"On the back of the picture was an inscription." Meghan checked her notebook. "'Bráithreachas Phoblacht na hÉireann,'" she said. "Do you know what that means?"

He shrugged and mumbled something that sounded like, "I don't have a clue what you're talking about."

"As I remember," she said, "it means 'Irish Republican Brotherhood.' If he was in this picture, was your grandfather involved?"

"Of course, he wasn't connected. At that time my grandfather's clients were British officials, like Lord Aberdeen's wife and the wives of other Englishmen in the administration. He would never have allowed politics to do damage to his reputation."

"No. I'm sorry. Didn't mean to speak ill of your grand-father. As you're a jeweler, I have a question. If someone stole the Crown Jewels, how would they get money in return?"

With a nervous smile, he said, "Hypothetically, someone might travel to Antwerp. That city is the undisputed gemstone capital of the world, a global trading hub. There were at least one hundred trading companies in operation at that time; not all were legit."

Meghan said, "At the time the jewels were stolen, it is estimated the monetary value would have been around 33,000 pounds—approximately 4 million to 5 million today. What do you think the people in Antwerp would pay?"

Girrard shook his head in exasperation. "I don't know. Maybe 30,000."

She held her iPhone up. "Mrs. Cosgrove said the man in the center's name was James Connally. Do you know who he was?"

"No," he said, avoiding eye contact. Meghan saw that Girrard was surprised and uneasy. She knew he was lying.

"Thank you, sir, for your help."

Outside the jewelry store, she browsed Google's search engine and found that James Connally was an Irish Republican, executed for his part in the 1916 Easter Rising against British rule in Ireland.

Bloody hell, Meghan thought. Mary O'Farrell hated Vicars, and she was affiliated with the secret Republican group Bráithreachas Phoblacht na hÉireann.

It all snapped into place. Mary O'Farrell had stolen the Irish Crown Jewels.

...28

BLACK MONDAY

DURING THE SUMMER, MEGHAN continued working as a freelance journalist, handling criminal proceedings in District Court for the *Times*. Mr. Eamonn Duggan, her newspaper editor, was a relic of a bygone era, crusty and foul-tempered. His vocabulary consisted mostly of grumbles, curses, and barked orders. He had no patience for sentimentality, or anything that wasn't a hard-hitting story. His insults were sharp as a razor, his criticisms brutal. "If it bleeds, it leads," he told Meghan.

At night and on weekends, she managed to complete her book, *The Cleaning Woman's Secret*. After the final editing, Meghan went to the Business Depot on Harold Cross Road. They provided her with a bound copy to present to her publisher, Deirdre McAuley, owner of the Beacon Press.

It was another week before Deirdre McAuley telephoned. "Meghan. My dear, this one is not for us," she said. "There is some fragment of truth, but it's more fiction than non-fiction."

"Jesus, Deirdre. It's an exposé. Mary O'Farrell really stole the Crown Jewels. She gave them to James Connally, the Republican leader in Dublin. Connally took the jewels to Antwerp to get money for arms—"

Her publisher broke in. "Do you have evidence of that?"

"No. It's my theory. A gut reaction."

"Your theory," Deirdre McAuley snorted. "Where did you get the information?"

"I interviewed Mary O'Farrell's 98-year-old granddaughter, Emer Cosgrove."

"Honey, 98-year-old people make up stories to fill gaps in their reminiscences. Since the Official Secrets Act was annulled, other authors have been involved in analyzing the unsolved jewel crime. The Town House Press published *The Stealing of the Irish Crown Jewels,* and Collins Press handled *Scandal and Betrayal.* Sorry, dear. Your book is not for us. No one needs *another* Crown Jewels story."

Meghan felt surprised and speechless. When the call was completed, she muttered, "Fucking hell." Then her phone buzzed again. Donna Maguire, secretary to Brendan McFarlane, was on the phone.

"Meghan," she said. "I have sad news. Mr. McFarlane died."

A quick suck of breath from Meghan, and then silence.

*   *   *

WHEN MEGHAN ARRIVED AT THE *Times* newspaper, there was grief and despondency. At eleven o'clock, a moment of silence honored Brendan McFarlane's memory. His journalism career spanned 50 years, including nearly two decades at the *Irish Times.* McFarlane had been awarded the Irish Journalism Award three times.

Meghan remembered Brendan McFarlane as a friend. After she wrote the story offending the Official Secrets Act, she had been imprisoned for six months. After she served her time, Managing Director McFarlane welcomed her back to the *Times.*

"God rest his soul," she said.

Late in the day, her editor, Eamonn Duggan, called her into his office. Duggan had a broad bulldog face, with a prominent nose, graying hair, and big eyes behind solid-framed spectacles. His office reeked of stale coffee, cigarettes, and the faint, musty scent of newsprint. He hitched up his trousers and leaned back in his desk chair, plump hands linked across his generous stomach. He smiled, but it wasn't a real smile: just a tightening of the flesh across his lips.

"Have a seat," he said and waved her to a chair.

She offered him a brittle smile and sat down on a chair in his office. Meghan noticed he was staring at her breasts for too long, and too often. She thought, *He's hitting on me at a time like this.*

The silence stretched. Duggan pulled a squashed cigarette out of his shirt pocket and lit it. His mouth had an amused curl, like he was about to laugh at her. "I need to tell you, lass, the new managing director—will be me."

More luck to you, she thought.

"I need to ask you a few questions," Duggan said. "Instead of being a reporter, would you like to be a sub-editor?"

Her body tensed. "Yes, of course."

"Ah, sure that's grand." Duggan gave a harsh laugh. "I've heard woman with red hair have higher sexual desire. Is that true?"

Meghan stiffened in her seat. She lifted her eyebrows. "Are you talking about having sex with me?"

Duggan wore an expression that said *what else?* "One hand washes the other," he said. "If I get what I want, then you will get what you want."

Meghan winced in disgust at his comment. She felt a tremor of disquiet but shrugged it off. "And if I say no?"

There was an edge to Duggan's voice. "If you say *no*, then perhaps it's best for you to find employment elsewhere."

A flare of uncontrollable fury shot through her. Meghan took a deep breath; now was the moment of reckoning. She gave him a look of withering contempt. "Get fucked, Duggan. You're a dirty bastard."

Duggan gave an outraged snort. His face flushed with anger. He leaned forward, hands clenched on the edge of his desk, a patchy fever-red flush coming up on his cheekbones. "Get out. You're fired."

...29

E-MAIL

SATURDAY MORNING, MEGHAN HAD THOUGHT her book about Mary O'Farrell would change everything. Instead, it joined the graveyard of "Unfortunately, we must pass on it," as Deirdre McAuley had told her. And with that news from her publisher, the same day she was fired from the *Irish Times*.

When Brendan McFarlane was alive, he'd promised Meghan her job was stable. Now, with no paycheck and a lease she couldn't afford, she was out of options. If she couldn't get a new job soon, the thought of calling her mother—her remarried, ever-critical mother—made her stomach turn. Their relationship had always been strained, a dance of unspoken disappointments and clipped conversations. She could already hear her mother's sighs, the passive-aggressive remarks about life choices, the underlying "I told you so" in every word. But pride wouldn't pay her rent.

Meghan had thought she was launching a writing career. Instead, at 35, she felt like she was moving backward, maybe returning to a house that, after her father died, had never felt like home. If she did that, it would mean carrying the weight of failure. A tear crept into Meghan's eye.

Almost on impulse, Meghan felt she had to reduce her anxiety. Jogging was her preferred choice. A 5K run stimulated the release of endorphins and offered her a chance to reset mentally. Meghan took a light rain-resistant jacket and tied it around her waist in case of drizzle, pairing it with running leggings and trainers that had seen many miles. Before she left, she checked her email.

To: MegWalsh@gmail.com
Subject: FYI
From: Dr. Bryce Hardy

Dear Meghan:

Saw a show on TGA about Mary O'Farrell's granddaughter. Mary was the one who cleaned the Office of Arms and discovered the jewels were missing. You should interview her for your book.
Regards,
Bryce
Dr. Bryce Hardy
Curator, Dublin Castle
BHardy @live.com

Megan responded:

BHardy @live.com
Subject: No Joy!
From: MegWalsh@gmail.com

Dear Bryce:

Thank you. I already interviewed Emer Cosgrove, the granddaughter of Mary O'Farrell. It was revealing. I believe it was Mary who stole the Crown Jewels. I'm sending you a picture that I took in Emer Cosgrove's home. The man on the second left was Mary's son, Seamus, and the one in the center was James Connally, executed for his part in the 1916 Easter Rising. The man on the second right was Mr. Girrard, a jeweler.

I checked the back of the picture. Bráithreachas Pdoblacht na hÉireann was inscribed. The one you told me about, the Brotherhood of the Republic of Ireland, the secret organization that fought for Ireland's independence from Great Britain.

My belief is Mary or Seamus O'Farrell had the Crown Jewels and gave them to James Connally. He took the jewels to Antwerp and cashed them in to get arms. I wrote all of that in my book.

Deirdre McAuley, my publisher, said, "This one is not for us. There is some fragment of truth, but it's more fiction than non-fiction. Old people make up stories to fill gaps in their recollection. No one needs another Crown Jewels fiction story."

I was also fired from my job at the *Times*. My friend, Director Brendan McFarlane, died, and the new boss, a dirty bastard named Duggan, wanted me to "drop my drawers" to keep my job. Now, I have no job, no publisher, and no rent payment. So yesterday was really a shitstorm.

Almost immediately she received another message.

To: MegWalsh@gmail.com
Subject: Sorry
From: Dr. Bryce Hardy

Dear Meghan:

Sorry to hear the bad news. The truth is, you are a good writer and reporter. I've read your accounts in the *Times* and loved your book *The House of Sleep*. Take a deep breath. Consider applying to either the *Irish Independent*,

Irish Examiner or the *Evening Herald*. I may have other suggestions. Will get back to you later.

Be of good cheer.

Bryce

Dr. Bryce Hardy

Curator, Dublin Castle

BHardy @live.com

*   *   *

MEGHAN JOGGED ALONG THE leafy paths of Poppintree Park, her breath steady in the crisp morning air. The city was waking up around her; buses hummed along the quays. Occasionally, she nodded to fellow joggers or dodged a cyclist. The distant chiming of church bells and the scent of fresh rain on cobblestones mixed with the earthy aroma of the park. Her hair, a cascade of fiery red, fell in waves over her shoulders, catching the light like autumn leaves ablaze. She simply enjoyed the rhythm of her run, the Dublin air filling her lungs as she pushed forward, feeling less anxious, remembering what Bryce Hardy had said: "Be of good cheer."

After she returned home, she showered, dressed, and had breakfast: a cup of tea and a slice of crispbread with cream cheese. Her phone buzzed.

"Meghan Walsh?" The caller asked.

"No, I don't want to buy—anything."

She heard a man clearing his throat. "My friend, Dr. Bryce Hardy, suggested I call you. My name is Jason Finn. I'm the publisher of Wolfhound Press."

"I'm sorry, Mr. Finn. I didn't mean to sound a total shit."

"We all get unwanted calls." He continued, "Our firm publishes for the non-fiction market; our range of subjects also includes biography, politics, history, and crime. Bryce told me you had written a book unraveling the theft of the Crown Jewels from Dublin Castle in 1907. Is that correct?"

"Yes, it's *The Cleaning Woman's Secret.* I believe that Mary O'Farrell, or maybe her son, Seamus, was responsible. It's circumstantial. I have no evidence."

Finn replied, "Absence of evidence is not evidence of absence. It means, just because you haven't found proof of something doesn't necessarily mean it doesn't exist. Dr. Hardy said your research was linked to the Bráithreachas Phoblacht na hÉireann. If they were involved, that's quite a story to tell."

A bracing burst of adrenaline shot through her.

"Tell me about your writing," Finn said.

"My book *The House of Sleep* won second prize in a contest last year for non-fiction. This year I was trying with *The Cleaning Woman's Secret* for the An Post Irish Book Awards for Non-Fiction. The close of submission date is 20 August, but I have no publisher."

A moment of quiet.

Jason Finn said, "There is still time before the 20th, but I would need to review your book, talk to my editors, and meet with you—if that's possible."

Impulsively she said, "Why not tonight?"

Finn paused. "Where can we meet? Your choice."

"How about the Gravediggers, a pub in Glasnevin on Prospect Square?"

He was very quiet. Wry. "Sounds kind of ghoulish."

"Just a lovely, quiet bar," Meghan told him. "And it's near my home. How about six o'clock?"

"Sounds good," Jason replied. "See you there."
Meghan sighed in relief. She wiped away a tear.

...30

THE GRAVEDIGGER'S PUB

THE PUB WAS LOCATED right next to the Glasnevin Cemetery. The interior had remained largely unchanged since its early days, with low ceilings, wood-paneled walls, and a proper snug where you could enjoy a quiet pint. Two hurleys, the wooden stick used in the Irish sport of hurling, were crisscrossed over a blotched mirror. Above them was a triple frame. It showed the pope, St. Patrick, and John F. Kennedy's picture in the center. *The Irish saints.*

As Meghan arrived, her eyes adjusted to the sudden cave-like darkness of the pub. She went right up to the bar. "Guinness, please."

The barkeep, a round-faced guy, said, "On the house." He smiled. "We don't take money from pretty women like you. It's good for business."

"Do you hire them?"

He gave her a sharp glance. "What do you mean?"

"I lost my job. I need to find work. What do you pay?"

His neck shot red. "You're fooling with me. Do you think I'm an eejit?" He ignored her, pretending urgent business at the other end of the bar.

Meghan took her pint to the back, near the fireplace, where she found it was quiet, with only moderate conversation in the background. She downed a second Guinness to calm her nerves.

Just after six o'clock, Jason Finn bounced in. He was somewhere in his forties, small and wiry, friendly, with bushy eyebrows and a thick handlebar mustache. He spotted Meghan, then put up a finger and went to the bar.

When Finn returned, he said, "You must be Meghan."

"Indeed, yes. How did you know?"

"Bryce Hardy said you would be of medium height, with green eyes and a shock of bright red hair, and the most striking woman in the bar. I couldn't miss."

"If this hasn't just about made my day," Meghan said, feeling groggy, the stout heavy on her stomach.

Jason Finn looked around. "I've never been here."

"It's next to a cemetery. That's why it's called the Gravedigger's Pub. Back in the eighteen hundreds, the cemetery's gravediggers would stop by for a pint or two. The pub's side entrance opened directly onto the cemetery and made it easy for the gravediggers to slip in and out unnoticed. Over time, the nickname stuck."

Meghan noticed he had no ring. She seriously needed to do something about her social and sexual life. Her sexual relationship was satisfying, but sinful. She had a casual relationship with a defense lawyer at the Dublin Criminal Courts office. The lawyer was married and not often available.

At home alone, she would look forward to eating a frozen dinner in front of her TV. *Loneliness is hard*, she mused. *It's one of the big ones.*

"So, tell me about you," Jason said.

"I'm still above ground, breathing, and half drunk."

His jaw tightened. "Maybe a little more information?"

She rested a finger on the rim of her glass. "It's a long story."

"I've got all night."

Meghan gazed at him. *All night.* Her thoughts descended into carnal oblivion. There was a moment of silence. Meghan took another long pull of stout and felt it hit the right button. She recrossed her legs, noticing she was wet.

Through her fog of drink, she said, "You're an attractive man. If you're my publisher, can we have a... relationship?"

Jason Finn downed his beer. "I'd like to think about that offer, but first, I need to talk to my partner. He may not agree."

Meghan mused, *He's gay.*

"My bad. I wasn't expecting—"

Jason interrupted, "Is that a problem?"

Meghan was jolted back, transitioning from her precoital eagerness. "Ah, no, for fuck's sake," she snorted. "I accept people for who they are, people like you who make me feel valued and not bring me down."

At first, he looked a little skeptical, then smiled and nodded. "Well spoken. Tell me about your writing."

There was moment of silence. "I married my husband, Matthew Walsh, in 2014. He was a foreign correspondent for *The Irish Times.* Unfortunately, Matt developed a terminal illness."

"I'm sorry," Jason said.

She took a deep breath. "Following my husband's death, I worked for the *Times* as an investigative journalist until 2020. Then I was imprisoned for six months for offending the British Official Secrets Act. My story revealed that police had prior knowledge of the 2009 Bank of Ireland robbery, where 7.6 million euro was stolen from the College Green cash center in Dublin. My story created a stir. I was arrested, along with my *Times* managing director, Brendan McFarlane. He paid a fine, and I went to jail."

"More luck to him." Finn shook his head.

"After serving my time in prison, I decided I wanted to write books, not newspaper crime stories. Director McFarlane owed me a favor. He allowed me time to work on my writing in the morning. Then in the afternoon, I continued working freelance at the *Times*, handling criminal proceedings in Dublin's District Court."

Jason raised one eyebrow. "Perhaps a little more?"

Meghan continued, "I have a one-bedroom unit. Matt's 250,000-euro life insurance policy provided me 2000 per month for the last few years. With my freelance reporting I can earn another 10,000 to 12,000 euro per year. But now that I've been fired..." She rolled her eyes and sighed. "I've got no income. It's shite."

"Why did you get fired?"

Meghan turned her pint mug in her hands. "Ah, well, I was fired after refusing to sleep with my boss."

A puff of laughter burst out of Jason Finn. "Good for you."

Her shoulders stiffened, almost imperceptibly. "Not so good. If I can't work at other newspapers, I may have to wait on tables here."

"From what I hear," Jason grinned, "a waitress in a Dublin bar can expect to earn around 13 euro per hour on average; however, other income is derived from tips, depending on how friendly she is with the customers."

"I know," Meghan said through gritted teeth. "And the men pat your arse—"

"Let's talk about your book," Jason interrupted. "That's why I'm here."

"So far, my leap into books is a dud. My *House of Sleep* book won second prize for non-fiction last year and I was awarded—a certificate. And now, my publisher doesn't think another unsolved Irish Crown Jewels robbery will sell."

Jason Finn had a trace of a smile. He took out a small notebook. "Bryce Hardy doesn't agree. I would like to read your *Cleaning Woman's Secret* myself. Can you summarize the key points?"

"It's not an Agatha Christie novel. I couldn't prove who really stole the jewels. From my crime investigation reporting days and Dr. Hardy's comments, I felt I could lay out the facts, as I knew them. I thought Lord Haddo was the thief, and then I got a big surprise."

"Seriously?"

"Yes. Now I'm convinced the cleaning lady, Mary O'Farrell, or her son were the thieves. When I visited Dr. Hardy at Dublin Castle, he told me about Bráithreachas Phoblacht na hÉireann, a secret organization dedicated to the establishment of an Independent Democratic Republic in Ireland. It's possible this group stole the jewels to embarrass Lord Aberdeen, the King's Viceroy in Ireland. Aberdeen was a known nationalist and advocate for home rule.

"Then my *Times* director, McFarlane, told me about a news article about Mary O'Farrell's 98-year-old granddaughter. He encouraged me to meet her. Emer Cosgrove was a nice lady, gave me tea and awful scones. Mrs. Cosgrove had photos on her wall, and with permission I snapped a picture of a group of men. She showed me her son, Seamus, was in the picture, and the man in the center she identified as James Connally, executed for his part in the 1916 Easter Rising against British rule. I looked on the back of the picture, and handwritten was 'Bráithreachas Phoblacht na hÉireann.'"

"Impressive."

"In addition," Meghan told Jason, "another man in the picture was a noted jeweler, Mr. Girrard. It's my theory, the one that I wrote in my book, that Connally took the jewels to where Mr. Girrard told him... to Antwerp. There, I'm certain, he took the money and bought guns. End of story."

"Meghan," he said through his cigarette, cupping his flame. "I'm on board."

Her sadness vanished. They clinked glasses and took another drink.

...31

THE AWARDS

IN AUGUST, WOLFHOUND PRESS published Meghan's book, *The Cleaning Woman's Secret*. The book was in time for the 20 August submission close date for the An Post Irish Book Awards.

In the meantime, through a connection from Wolfhound publisher Finn, Meghan was hired by the *Irish Independent*, the largest selling daily newspaper in Ireland, often seen as a good alternative to the *Irish Times*. For a few months, Meghan worked full time for the paper while on the weekends she attended either the Temple Bar Market or the St. Stephen's Green Market, setting up a stall to sell her two books directly to customers.

On 24 October the *Irish Times* listed the winners for the An Post Irish Book Awards. The WHSmith Non-Fiction Book of the Year went to *Missing Persons, Or My Grandmother's Secrets*—Clair Wills, Penguin Random House, publisher. Meghan's book wasn't mentioned for the second or third prize.

Her book *The Cleaning Woman's Secret* not being named for any of the awards was a profound hurt, an agonizing erosion of her talent as a writer. Her publisher, Jason Finn, tried to console her. "Your story of an elderly cleaning woman stealing the Irish Crown Jewels was difficult for the An Post Irish jury to believe. You offered no proof, no evidence, no confession. In addition, it was bad timing. They also had another grandmother's secrets book to choose from—"

"Oh, bugger," Meghan interrupted. "The old cleaning lady really did it."

"Yeah," Jason said, a little dryly. "Your book is on Amazon and Kindle. It may be more popular with the American readers. Let me pour you a nice, cold, refreshing glass of reality. With most publishers' new books, eighty percent fail, and the twenty percent that succeed pay for all the failures."

Meghan nodded. She supposed that made sense.

He added, "You're a good writer—not Tana French or Sally Rooney, but I see a talent, and I'll make you a proposal, a novel that could win you the Booker award."

"Pray tell."

Jason asked, "Is Ireland headed for a merger?"

Meghan shrugged and said, "How would I know?"

"With Catholics now outnumbering Protestants in Northern Ireland," he said, "advocates for unification believe their dream can become a reality. It's closer now than it's ever been. The referendum would reignite old enmities. That's the novel I want to publish—the love story between a Protestant and a Catholic."

With a faint smile, she said, "A Romeo and Juliet story? That didn't work out well. They died by suicide."

"Don't be foolish," Jason advised. "Love, passion, conflict, fate, and tragedy are universal human experiences. Even though *Romeo and Juliet* was written over 400 years ago, people still connect to those feelings today. It adds tension and excitement because readers want to see whether the couple will overcome the obstacles."

"No. I'm sorry. I have no heart for any more Irish politics."

Jason persisted, "With this novel you might win the Booker Prize award for the best full-length novel written in English and published in the UK and Ireland. The Booker award winner receives 50,000 pounds."

Meghan thought, *£50,000 Booker prize money*. Her husband's insurance policy was running out, and she couldn't afford her apartment with her salary from the *Irish Independent*. She asked, "Jason, can I think about it?"

She heard a deep sigh. "Please don't dawdle. Call me tomorrow, yes or no." Then Jason Finn abruptly hung up.

...32

THE PACKAGE

THE FOLLOWING MORNING Meghan found a small package at her door delivered by DTDC Australia. As she unwrapped the parcel, she found a note and a large notebook. She then read a letter from an attorney in Sydney, Australia.

Dear Ms. Walsh,

My name is Raymond Gilmour. I am a solicitor associated with Gilmour & O'Dea Lawyers, Sydney. I am the executor of the estate of one of our clients, Mrs. Dessie Ellis. Her family came from Ireland.

She was a widow with no children. Mrs. Ellis had a safe custody vault in the Commonwealth Bank of Australia. It was my responsibility to empty the contents of the vault after her death. There were stocks and bonds certificates that had value, and funds donated, according to her will, to the Salvation Army. Also, I found a large notebook. Apparently, it was written by Mrs. Ellis's grandfather.

Ms. Walsh, when I read your book, *The Cleaning Woman's Secret*, on Kindle, I felt it was my duty to deliver this information to you. You were wrong. Mary O'Farrell never stole the Irish Crown Jewels.

...33

FINAL JOURNAL

MY NAME IS OWEN KERR. I was born in Dún Laoghaire, Ireland in 1865. Now I'm in my eighties, and in the final stage of my kidney disease, I felt it important to journal the actual events of the Irish Crown Jewels robbery in the year 1907.

When Scotland Yard Inspector John Kane came to Ireland to investigate the theft on 11 July, I went to my Commissioner, John Ross, and said we had gotten nowhere on this robbery. I requested to work with the Scotland Yard inspector, saying if we can clear up this robbery, then your Metropolitan Police will also get the credit.

I closely observed Inspector John Kane's questioning of suspects. He was knowledgeable and experienced. I felt in a few more days, he was going to get somewhere, perhaps to Lord Haddo and myself. That was unacceptable, and I confided to Sir John Ross that Inspector Kane had evidence that Sir Arthur Vicars entertained men known as practicing homosexuals at his home and that at these parties, the King's brother-in-law, the Duke of Argyll, made a habit of attending. The information obviously got to Lord Aberdeen; the following day John Kane was dismissed from the case, and he returned to London.

I'll tell you my motives. Ireland had been under British control since the Norman invasion in the late 12th century. Many Irish Catholics, like my grandparents

150

and cousins, who formed the majority in Ireland, faced discrimination. My father was a famous police officer with unionist ties.

I felt a deep resentment of the British rule. But when I came to Dublin and joined the Metropolitan Police, I was stationed in Dublin Castle, the main British outpost in Ireland, and my job was to patrol the damnable castle at night and make sure all was in order.

When I heard that the King was coming to Dublin, I thought if I stole the Crown Jewels from the safe in the library, the British King would be humiliated. Even more than that, he would have to get rid of Sir Arthur Vicars, the pompous fool in charge of the Office of Arms and the Crown Jewels. Vicars treated staff who worked for him as indentured servants, including me as well. So, I was laying a trap for him.

I needed Lord Haddo to assist me. I told Haddo I was prepared to go to the press and name him as a practicing homosexual, along with the King's brother-in-law. That news would have required his father, as the King's Lord Lieutenant of Ireland, to resign, and the family would have been disgraced. Haddo caved, as I knew he would. I instructed Haddo to get the safe key for me from the bedroom when Vicars had had too much to drink and was sleeping. Then, I immediately substituted a similar key, and Haddo returned my fake key to Vicars's bedroom.

Then I sent Lord Haddo to Scotland for an alibi, if need be. During my nightly inspection on 3 June, I emptied the Crown Jewels and the collars. I had Vicars's key to the safe and my own key to the strongroom. On the night of 6 June, I opened the safe and the strongroom lock to be sure the theft was discovered before the King came to Ireland. When the theft was discovered, I suggested to Commissioner Ross that I should go with Vicars and get the safe key for evidence. He agreed. Then I replaced the original safe key and turned it over to Ross.

After John Kane was forced out, I waited for a month; then I resigned from the Metropolitan Police. I told Commissioner Ross that the Royal Commission and Sir David Harrel still considered it my dereliction of duty that had caused the theft. I felt my career in the police was over. I think Ross was relieved.

I went back to my home in Dún Laoghaire. My parents died and willed me the house. I sold it and told the neighbor that with the money from the home sale, I wanted to travel to Europe. In October, I went to Antwerp. There were many trading companies in operation; some were not lawful, and I was able to collect £35,000 for the jewels.

I then headed overseas to Australia. With my fundings, I started the first security guard company in Australia, the Sydney Night Patrol. I married and had two sons and a daughter. My eldest son, Lieutenant Denis Kerr, was killed in the second war during the fighting in the jungles of New Guinea against the Japanese. I don't know where Denis is buried.

My other son, Sean, was too young for the war. He left Australia and moved to America. Boston. My daughter, Dessie, married a decent guy, Patrick Ellis, a schoolteacher. They live nearby in Sydney. After my wife died of cancer, I was a mess. Dessie managed everything. Even now, she handles my banking, shopping, and my pills. My doctor said, "Your infection has moved to your bloodstream. A sepsis might occur, which can lead to your death, within a few days or weeks."

As such, I'm writing my final journal. With my signature, I confess I personally stole the Irish Crown Jewels.

Yours,

Owen Kerr

09 January 1947

...34

THE SEQUEL

MEGHAN BREATHED IN A SIGH as she read the letter from the Sydney solicitor. The corners of her mouth tightened up. "Ah, Jesus, it was Detective Kerr."

It was coming up to six p.m. when she checked her watch and found it was five a.m. in Sydney, NSW, Australia. Too early to call. She checked Gilmour's internet address and wrote an email.

To: Raymond Gilmour @raygilmour.com.au.
14 August 2025

Dear Mr. Gilmour:

Thank you for the package you sent to me containing your letter and Owen Kerr's confession. I made a mistake in my book. A bad one. Mary O'Farrell never stole the Crown Jewels. Now that I know what happened, I'd like to write a sequel. I don't wish to be involved in any copyright problems, so I would like to ask if I can proceed with my non-fiction project? Thank you again for sending me the information.
Meghan Walsh
Email: Megwalsh@independent.ie

THE NEXT MORNING, Meghan got a reply.

To: MegWalsh@independent.ie
15 August 2025

Dear Ms. Walsh,

Owen Kerr committed a crime. You are more than welcome to include his confession in your sequel. I will look forward to reading it on Kindle.

Best wishes,

Raymond Gilmour

*   *   *

FOLLOWING THE EMAIL EXCHANGE, Meghan called Jason Finn.

"What did you decide?"

She felt an irrational little stir of panic in her stomach. "I don't want to write the novel you suggested about an Irish Romeo and Juliet romance."

A short, suspicious pause. "Why?"

"I received a parcel from a lawyer in Australia. In it was a final journal from detective Owen Kerr, who before his death, confessed to stealing the Crown Jewels."

"Are you fucking serious, no messing with me?"

"Serious as a heart attack. I am, yeah," Meghan said. "I want to write a sequel for the next Booker award."

A silence hung in the air.

"Fair play," Jason finally said. "If it's good, I'll publish it. What's the title?"

That slow, wide, beautiful smile spread across Meghan's face. She said, "Thanks, that's grand.

"It's called *STOLEN*."

...Epilogue

THE ENDURING MYSTERY

ON 30 JANUARY 1908, SIR ARTHUR VICARS'S appointment as Ulster King of Arms was terminated. Believing he had been made a scapegoat for the jewels, he retired, embittered. He was shot outside his home by a local IRA unit in April 1921.

Also in April 1921, Francis Goldney died in a motoring accident in France. His effects were found to include ancient charters and documents belonging to the City of Canterbury and other works of art.

Pierce Gun Mahoney was shot through the heart in 1914 in what appeared to be a hunting accident. For Francis Richard Shackleton, the shadow of suspicion stalked him for the rest of his life. He died at St Richard's Hospital on 24 June 1941, at age 64, and was buried, under the name of Mellor, in Chichester cemetery.

Chief Inspector John Kane remained at Scotland Yard until he retired in December 1911, after 37 years' service. Although the Kane report has never been made public (Scotland Yard to this day denies its existence), we can glean important inferences from his testimony. Kane suggested that the thief was a castle insider, with more right to be in the Office of Arms than himself. The thief's motive was to create a great embarrassment prior to the King's visit.

By mentioning a forged key, Kane implied that Sir Arthur was not the thief.

He also vouched for the innocence of Shackleton. We know that the Irish administration was most distressed over the suspect named in Kane's report and dismissed the Chief Inspector. The person he named in his report must have had considerable stature in Ireland. Mahoney was not a man of any stature, nor was Goldney, who was just an English mayor. Only one remaining person associated with Sir Arthur had the stature and prestige to compel the Irish administration and the Lord Lieutenant to go to such extreme lengths to shield him; that person was Lord Haddo. He generally escaped the Crown Jewels fiasco unscathed.

The story of the Crown Jewels is as much a story about Sir Arthur Vicars as the jewels themselves. While I would not espouse his politics, the man shines forth from the pages of history as a gentleman, more interested in scholarly pursuits than worldly affairs, and as often as not, willing to do a fellow human being a good turn. The final rebuke to all who deceived him came from his wife, Lady Vicars, who lies interred beside him: she added the inscription to her tombstone, "Faithful to the end."

The original safe from which the jewels were stolen now sits, largely redundant, in a corner of the lost and stolen property office in Kevin Street Garda Station in Dublin. It bears the legend "Ratner Safe—Thief Proof."

The fate of the Irish Crown Jewels remains an unsolved mystery.

Appendix

THE IRISH CROWN JEWELS

THE REGALIA OF THE IRISH CROWN JEWELS refers to the insignia of the chivalric Order of St. Patrick, established by the British monarchy in 1783 to honor the Irish aristocracy. These jewels were considered the Irish equivalent of the English Order of the Garter and the Scottish Order of the Thistle.

THE GRAND MASTER'S DIAMOND STAR

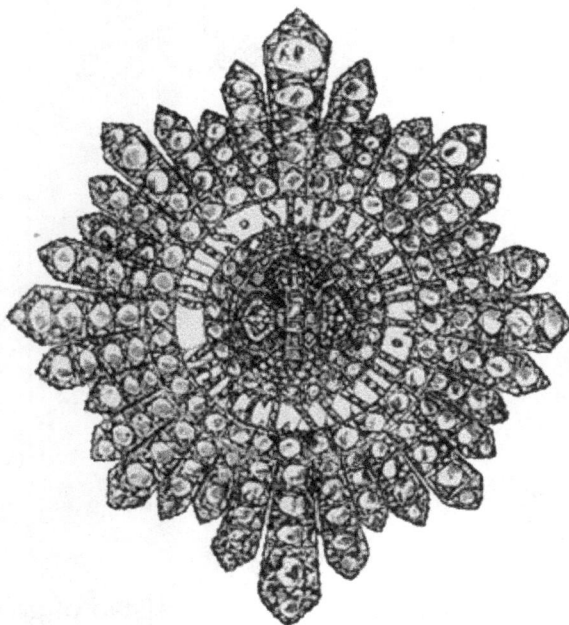

A diamond-studded badge (or star): This was the main piece of the collection, made of Brazilian diamonds, emeralds, and rubies set in silver and gold. It featured a shamrock motif and a cross of St. Patrick.

COLLAR BADGE OF KNIGHT COMPANION

The diamond-studded collars consisted of gold harps (symbolizing Ireland) and knots, with a central St. Patrick's Cross.

GRAND MASTER'S DIAMOND BADGE

A jeweled pendant, a significant piece attached to the collar, was stored in the strongroom of the Office of Arms. In 1907, these jewels were valued at £33,000. The Regalia of the Irish Crown Jewels would be worth about $20 million today.

Author's Note

DURING THE LAST 26 YEARS, I've enjoyed the pleasure of writing. Some of my books are historical fiction. To research these books, my passion for this genre has taken me to Chorwon, Korea; Venice and Milan, Italy; Kyoto, Japan; Chantilly, France; Kiryat Shmona, Israel; and Yangzhou, China.

Historical fiction appeals to people who love a good story, are curious about the past, and appreciate the rich blend of reality and imagination this genre offers. My books may inspire both chills and serious thought. Historical fiction may not always stick strictly to documented events, but its essence lies in telling an emotional or philosophical truth.

I would like to thank the four people who have given me such expert advice and assistance for years: my readers, Jeff Dobson and Peter Haase; my editor, Jennifer Adkins; and my graphic designer, Scott Mahr.

As always, any inaccuracies, deliberate or otherwise, are mine.

Malcolm Mahr
Vero Beach, Florida
May 2025

Look for Mr. Mahr's next book:

Malcolm Mahr's books are available to order
at macmahr.com or Amazon.com.